MISTRESS FOR HIRE

ABBY PARKER

◆ FriesenPress

Suite 300 - 990 Fort St
Victoria, BC, V8V 3K2
Canada

www.friesenpress.com

ISBN
978-1-5255-3365-5 (Hardcover)
978-1-5255-3366-2 (Paperback)
978-1-5255-3367-9 (eBook)

1. FICTION, ROMANCE, CONTEMPORARY

Distributed to the trade by The Ingram Book Company

This book is dedicated to our inner voice.

May she continue to come through as
authentic, loud, clear, and strong.

May we continue to do her proud.

Chapter 1
The Bartender

I'D FINALLY EXPERIENCED WHAT ALL MY FRIENDS raved about—the hook up, the one-night stand, and I'd loved it!

Nestling into Josh's well-defined chest, I savored the feeling, enjoying our fleeting moments together. He was a respectful and sweet lover, had an old-fashioned way about him, but I'd heard through the rumor mill he was a player, not a keeper. It would never work. He'd probably grow tired of me after a week.

Enjoying the warmth of his body, I shifted through foggy thoughts, recalling how we'd met and more importantly, how I'd ended up in his bed! He was a regular at the coffee shop and we usually chatted while I prepared his order. He was polite, attractive and had a way with words.

One day, handing him an espresso, he slid his business card across the counter, "The Chic Chick" written in bold pink. "See you tonight at the club?" I knew he was a bartender. I was overdue for an evening out—that night we became friends.

I'd become a regular at his club and was finishing a martini, deflecting the advances of an attractive stranger wanting to buy me a drink. He was probably the sixth one that night. I'd lost count. Despite the barely existent funds in my bank account, thanks to my low paying job at the coffee shop, I'd graciously refused his offer. The tan line on his wedding finger showed he was married or recently separated - problems. Plus, it was easier to buy my own drinks than trying to shake off any vultures coming to seek payment on their investment at the end of the night.

I was deep in thought over my finances, when Josh interrupted me. "So, Bree, was he the sixth or seventh guy to hit on you tonight? No one ever stands a chance with you, do they? The poor schmucks should just give up, but you're so damn beautiful I can't blame them." He placed his elbow on the edge of the bar, resting his chin on the back of his hand, emulating the infamous "Thinker" pose, and eyeballed me affectionately.

I blushed under his attention, then gently flicked my wrist in the air, chasing his compliment away. It was a running joke between us: how many men would I turn away in a night? Sometimes, we would make a game of it and bet. He would guess high and I would guess low. Josh usually won.

I placed my finger against my temple as if mulling it over. "I think he was number six."

"It was actually the seventh. I wanted to see if you were counting."

"I see you're watching over me again." I blew him a kiss then lifted my glass and tipped it upside down. "She's empty Josh. If you would be so kind as to fill her up again."

"No problem, Beautiful!" He took the glass from my hand and pinched my cheek. "You're simply adorable. I want to see those dimples. They seem to be in hiding tonight. I'll fix you up a nice stiff drink and cheer you up."

He looked at me, tilted his head with a questioning look, and said, "How can you still be single?" He turned and walked back to the bar.

His question was meant to be rhetorical, one he asked me often, one I had no *real* answer for. I was leery, I'd heard about a friend's venereal issue; adding to my desire to remain single. My mom's childhood preaching on the evils of sex also echoed through my head on occasion. Plus, truth be told, I hadn't really looked for any opportunities because at the time I didn't realize how great sex could be! I had never experienced an orgasm! I lost my virginity to my first official boyfriend, Sam, in the back seat of his parent's car. He was as awkward and unskilled as I, so I'd never had the pleasure of climaxing. The sex never improved, he started talking marriage and I wasn't even sure I liked him. He was a great guy, but I was too young to be thinking about marriage.

Perhaps I should expand my opportunities? I thought, admiring Josh's perfect buttocks and broad shoulders. *He's extremely hot himself.* Sitting on my perch, a high bar stool that didn't allow my feet to touch the floor. I felt like an eagle, looking down on its prey. I watched as he poured double the amount of alcohol he was supposed to.

3

My drink almost overflowing, he walked back, without spilling a drop. There was no question he was skilled at his job. "A martini for the most beautiful lady in New York!" he declared, bowing as if I were royalty, handing me the drink.

"Are you trying to get me drunk, handsome?" I gazed into his deep emerald eyes and toyed with the edge of my large hoop earing. I'd never flirted with Josh before, but I was so down and out over my dire financial situation I needed a boost.

"Are you flirting with me, Miss Bree?" He pretended to look shocked.

"Perhaps I am?" I shrugged, hoping I was coming off as nonchalant.

"Well, this is new," he chirped back, "and I like it."

Looking at the dance floor, I decided it was time to move. I was getting cold feet. I wasn't sure if I liked where this was heading. I'd heard Josh was a ladies' man and the idea of it didn't appeal to me!

Josh saw my hesitation and, being skilled at picking up women, didn't miss a beat. He took my hand so I couldn't run off, keeping me within his grasp.

"Stay with me. I enjoy your company. The next one is on me, and the one after that too," he said looking at me with an intensity he'd never shown before.

A faint tingling sensation developed between my legs. "I see. So, are you officially number eight?" I asked, looking downward, while I traced the rim of my glass, wanting to avoid his sexy gaze—it wasn't allowing me to think straight!

He laughed, "Yes, Miss Bree, I am now officially the eighth man to hit on you this evening. But will you accept my offer?"

My hand was still in his and I could feel the sexual tension building between us. I wasn't sure how I wanted the night to end, so I took a sip from my drink to help me decide. It was almost pure alcohol. I coughed at its strength, spraying some of the liquid onto his hand and interrupting our heated moment. He looked at me in surprise and then we both started to laugh.

Taking a napkin off the counter, I wiped his hand.

After clearing away my mess, he placed his other hand on mine, smiling he waited for an answer. I nodded.

"Really! That's a yes?"

I nodded again and he let out a loud holler. I was taken aback by his excitement. Several patrons turned, witnessing the commotion.

"Doesn't mean I can't change my mind by the end of the night," I said sternly, trying to play hard to get, but we both knew things were looking in his favor. My defiance was unlikely to last long.

"Believe me, Bree, I've watched you turn away countless men. You're stunning, and any man would be lucky to have you. I'm only asking you keep an open mind and consider it."

Then he leaned over the bar and pulled me in closer until our lips almost touched. "I have an idea. I'll make you a bet. There are two hours 'til closing. If I guess the exact amount of men to hit on you by the night's end, I get to take you home." His breath was sweet, and our lips touched ever so slightly as he spoke.

I could taste him. Feeling generous with my decision-making capabilities after several martinis, I shook his hand, accepting the offer.

He guessed two additional men would hit on me. It turned out to be three, but after drinking my last martini, I wanted him to win, so we fudged the numbers and I graciously and willingly accepted defeat. I'd already decided my first one-night stand was going to be with Josh. He was familiar to me and I secretly hoped his expertise would yield my first orgasm.

Chapter 2
The Chic Chick

I SQUIRMED, RELISHING THE THOUGHTS OF THE three amazing orgasms, generously indulged by Josh. He must have sensed I was awake and slowly opened his eyes, grinning at me, "Mornin' beautiful." His sexy voice, relaxed and sleepy.

I felt at ease wrapped in his arms. He pulled me closer and I nuzzled deeper into his embrace. The sexual release from our escapade had boosted the natural 'happy' chemicals in my blood stream; I was satisfied and pleased. Despite being our first time together, no awkwardness existed. He was an expert, well-practiced and accustomed to having women in his bed. Being a bartender at a popular nightclub had allowed him to become a veteran at such things.

Suddenly, I groaned and sat up in bed as a sobering picture came to mind. With regret in my voice, I thought out loud, "Did we use a condom?"

"No, it broke, remember. I only had the one and you begged me to keep going. You were an animal." He raised his eyebrows in approval.

Bringing my hand to my head, I gave my forehead a tap, confirming my stupidity. Without warning, I spat sour words his way, "I don't remember and it's clear you sleep around. Do I have anything I need to be concerned about?" I glared at him, as if he were already guilty. Hand in the cookie jar.

His grin turned to a frown and his shoulders slumped downward in disbelief. I'd insulted him. As he got out of bed, reaching for his pants, I was temporarily distracted by his toned, naked body, realizing then why I hadn't cared about the condom in my drunken state; he was gorgeous.

"You sure didn't seem to mind last night," he fired back, his voice coarse. "Besides, I know you don't sleep around, we've been friends long enough, so I risked it. I won't deny I've slept with several women, but I've used *precautions* with them . . . and to answer your question, no, you have nothing to worry about."

I flopped back down into the fluffy pillows, relieved to hear he was disease-free but apprehensive he might not be telling the truth. Our time together was officially over after my accusations, so I slipped out of bed, reclaiming the clothes I'd eagerly discarded all over the floor only hours earlier.

Easing by him, I used my garments to shield my naked body and headed to the bathroom to get dressed. The awkwardness was now in full swing and I no longer wished for him to see me naked.

I dressed quickly, then peeked my head out of the bathroom door; he was nowhere to be seen. *Good*, I thought. I couldn't get out of his apartment fast enough. Tiptoeing as quickly as I could, I made my way to the exit point. Turning the handle ever so slowly, I slipped through the front door.

Creak.

Damn! Did he hear that? I wondered, closing the door softly.

As I started down the hallway, I heard his apartment door open. He was smiling again. "What! You're not staying for breakfast?" he teased, trying to dispel the tension between us. It worked, and I smiled back. "You're a good person, Bree. I assure you, you have nothing to worry about. I would never do anything to jeopardize your well-being. Please believe me."

I knew then he was telling the truth. "Thanks, Josh. I appreciate your kind words. It definitely makes me feel better."

"Anything for you, Bree." He opened his door wider and tilted his head toward his apartment, motioning me inside. "Are you sure you don't want any pancakes? I make them from scratch. Plus, I've got whip cream." He grinned, a dimple appearing, imbedded in his left cheek. "For the pancakes and other things." He winked knowing I'd catch his drift.

Although I was famished from our shenanigans, I knew better than to enter his den for fear I might make *him* my breakfast. Shaking my head "No", I said, "See you next week at the club! And from now on, all bets are off!" I joked, lightening the mood even further before blowing a kiss his way. The elevator arrived, ready to scoop me away; I stepped inside, content our friendship was still intact.

*****

I was happy Josh and I were still friends, no strings attached. I looked forward to seeing him the following week at the club; his martinis were always the best! I didn't expect to talk to him until then so I was surprised when he called a couple of days later. He felt off about what happened and wanted to make it up to me.

My initial thought: he was trying to hook up again. But it didn't turn out to be the case. He was calling to ask if I wanted a job at the Chic Chick, the high-end club where he bartended. One of their servers was pregnant—they had a job opening. He knew I didn't care for my job at the coffee shop and wanted to help me out.

I was ecstatic! Josh had given me a great reference and the job was mine if I wanted it. I said yes on the spot! I was hired, and the owner hadn't even laid eyes on me. I started four days later.

Chapter 3
Happy Birthday

I FUMBLED IN MY OVERSIZED CREAM-COLORED purse, the edges of my lipstick container, sunglasses, and several other items tantalizing my fingertips before I grasped my keys. I plunged my house key into the lock and stepped inside, breathing deep as I enjoyed the scent of familiarity. Home at last, after an eight-hour shift waitressing at the ritzy downtown New York club, the Chic Chick.

I loved my job! Josh's referral had been a life changer for me! I'd been working at the club for almost four years already! I'd started at twenty-four: tall, thin, blue eyes, light golden brown hair, and a tight booty; these assets were a requirement for the job. The owner liked to please his thirsty customers with attractive staff. He bragged it helped increase his profit margins. The servers, myself included, were happy with the arrangement, as we made excellent tips.

Before that, working at a local coffee shop, I only got three shifts a week. The owner's wife didn't like the way her husband looked at me and punished me accordingly, limiting my shifts to the bare minimum. So, I'd picked up a second job selling beauty products. I didn't care for either job, but employment was scarce at the time; I took what was available. My financial situation was bleak, and I still lived with my parents. I had been lucky to stumble onto the job at the Chic Chick; sleeping with the head bartender had its advantages.

After four months of serving alcohol, I was able to move out of my parents' house and rent a condo. My mother was disappointed with my job choice, not wanting her only daughter working at a nightclub. Unexpectedly, she offered to pay all my expenses if I went to college, on the conditions I stay at home and quit my job, but I politely declined her generous offer. I was making too much money and wasn't willing to give it up. Besides, I had a couple friends with college degrees who were down and out, working jobs of similar caliber to the coffee shop. The job market wasn't good, and I was safer keeping my job at the Chic Chick. Life was good, and I wasn't about to sit in classes five days a week for a job that might not even exist once I'd finished my studies. I was doing just fine, happy to finally be living on my own, out from under my mother's wing.

I opened the fridge, peered inside, and found what I was looking for: a cold beer. I reached to the back, grabbing my reward by the neck and twisted off the cap. I was celebrating. I normally went to bed straight away, exhausted from an eight-hour shift, but it was my twenty-eighth birthday. I flopped onto the faux leather couch, littered with cushions of various sizes, and tossed off the three-inch heels. Taking a long sip, I closed my eyes and welcomed the quiet of my living quarters. No pounding music. No drunk patrons yelling for another beer. It was bliss. Setting the glass bottle on the wooden coffee table, I rubbed my sore feet for several minutes before flipping open the laptop.

An icon bounced up and down. I had messages. I clicked on it and a new post from Chloe, my best friend, popped up. She'd tagged me in a photo. She was smiling, her pearly whites on full display, and her niece and nephew, the twins, sat on either side of her. Their adorable faces and bright blue eyes smiled intently at a ginormous birthday cake, half pink and half blue, with two candles. Chloe looked happy sandwiched between them. I wondered then why she never wanted children. Many times before she'd said, "No rug rats for me." She was a good aunt and babysat the twins twice a month, but not a day more. She enjoyed their company but was happy to send them back to her brother by the end of the day.

I clicked on the comment button and wrote, "Charming." I'd barely removed my finger from the post button when my cell phone rang. An old photo of Chloe and I flashed on the screen, a picture of us as kids sitting on the porch swing, happily eating watermelon. I had linked the picture to her number, so it showed up every time she called.

"Hiya, beautiful." I smiled into the phone, knowing she'd hear the smile even if she couldn't see it.

"Oh, Bree, I miss you. I saw you posted a comment just now, I knew you'd still be up, and I wanted to give you a quick call. Quick because the twins are over, my time on the phone is limited. My twenty-eighth birthday is coming up next week. Can you come to Nova Scotia to help celebrate? Please, pretty please?"

I could almost see her big brown eyes shining and her lips pouting with a slight smile. She hadn't changed from when we were kids, wanting the last piece of watermelon on the plate. I'd always given in after the pouty lip came out.

I hesitated, mentally calculating what I'd made that night; it would easily pay for my flight to Nova Scotia. And I had a few days off.

"I'm not scheduled to work for the next three days. We could celebrate both of our birthdays." In a serious voice, trying to sound like a detective on a very important case, I declared. "Time is of the essence; I'll hop on the first available flight tomorrow."

"Excellent!" she squealed. "Hey, wait. It's your birthday?" Chloe rarely remembered anything that didn't benefit her, so I wasn't surprised she'd forgotten.

"Yes." I took another long sip of my cold beer, happy to be alone. "I'm celebrating right now."

"Do you have a man over to help out with the festivities?"

"No way. I'm enjoying a nice cold beer *by myself*. I've already had over forty men hit on me tonight. I've had enough male attention to last me a lifetime." I sighed. Trying to prove a point I had over exaggerated the number of admirers.

"Why don't you take the cute bartender for another *ride*?"

"What are you talking about?" I tried to sound angry. "I never should have told you about Josh!" Although we'd only hooked up the once and still remained friends to this day, almost four years later, Chloe often poked fun over the matter.

"Hooking up with him sure paid off. You've been rolling in cash ever since you rode him."

"Chloe, where are the kids?" I didn't want them to pick up her foul language. "They might hear you. Watch yourself."

"Oops! Thanks. OK back to my . . . um . . . I mean our birthday celebration plans. You get your little butt down to Nova Scotia first thing. We'll celebrate at the local pub. You know the one our parents went to when we were young. I think—" She stopped mid-sentence, interrupted by a loud cry in the background. "Damn, the kids are still up and probably fighting over the iPad again. I wish they'd just play together like we did as kids. I'll have to let you go. Should I call you back?"

"No, you've got your hands full. We can catch up later. I need to get some sleep, to make sure I'm rested enough to party with the likes of you," I teased.

"You're still as understanding and charming as always. Big hugs. Later, Babes."

"Later, Chloe Bear."

Her phone line was already dead, and I imagined her impatiently trying to discipline her niece and nephew, failing miserably.

Chapter 4
Chloe

WHEN I WAS FIVE, MY FAMILY MOVED TO CANADA from New York City. My mother had just turned forty and was going through a midlife crisis; she wanted a change. She got it . . . smack dab in the middle of Nova Scotia, Canada, in a small town called Bellevue. The year prior she'd watched an alluring show about Nova Scotia and was bound and determined to live there! Consequently, we moved!

Luckily, Dad had an excellent job as a technical consultant for a computer software firm, allowing him the freedom to work from home, giving us the opportunity to live almost any place in the world.

Bellevue was a friendly town where everyone knew each other. Living in rural Canada was completely different then New York and I quickly began to prefer our rural two-story home in Nova Scotia, with the wrap-around porch, to the crowded condo life in New York. That life didn't allow for porches or free spaces.

Our porch even had a swing and we often sipped Mom's homemade lemonade from it on sweltering summer days.

On one of those hot days, Chloe had accompanied her mother while dropping off some cookies at our new home. It was customary to bring new neighbors cookies, we were told. We were inseparable since that day, running and chasing each other, playing hide-and-go-seek underneath the porch. We also spent countless hours rocking in the swing, making many childhood memories. Chloe and I formed a strong friendship. We were not only friends, class-mates, and neighbors, we were like sisters.

We lived in Canada until I was thirteen. I naturally was upset when my mother announced she craved the city life once again and we were moving back to New York. She had never worked a day in her life, yet she made all the decisions. I often heard her complaining to my dad raising *children* was a full-time job, but I was their *only* child and not much work. Easy-going and carefree were my middle names and I made very few demands.

Once, when I was three, I'd dared to ask my mother for a baby sister. "Mommy, I want a sister now!" I bellowed, hands on my hips, face sour in defiance.

She was drinking a can of soda at the time, and she'd choked so hard on the dark liquid it sprayed all over the floor. That was my answer!

Although Mom didn't care much for children and got her way most of the time, she still had her ways of showing us we were loved. She would rub Dad's sore feet, read to me before bed and took care of us the best she could. She wasn't overly affectionate and because she didn't want the burden of another child, it ended up working in my favor. Mom felt sorry for me, having no siblings, so when I befriended

Chloe, she was often allowed to come over and play. Our friendship let Mom to ease up on her motherly duties; having her only child distracted with a new friend meant she didn't have to be my full-time playmate.

After my family moved back to New York, Chloe and I kept in touch through snail mail and the silly chain letters that were popular at the time. As the technical age took hold of the world we progressed to e-mail and social media as our means of contact. We had not seen each other since I moved; life always seemed to get in the way. Chloe's phone call was an unexpected but welcome surprise. I was looking forward to returning to our old neighborhood and catching up with my dear friend.

I also wanted to meet her husband. When they were married, I was working at the coffee shop and I'd pleaded with my parents to lend me money for the flight, but Mom would have nothing of it.

"Honey, you know we can't afford to fly you to Canada. I just purchased two matching treadmills!" She pointed a finger at the endless belt devices, on which she and my dad would walk or run in place for miles, testing their physiological abilities.

Upset with her lack of support, I frowned. "Why don't you just exercise outdoors? Instead of looking like two hamsters on a wheel?"

I knew I was being unfair and judgmental. I'd used treadmills before and enjoyed them, but as always, I felt she was just being self-centered.

She scoffed at my comments, waving them off like she would a fly. Mom was on a health kick, not interested in what I had to stay, and she was bringing poor Dad along for the ride. Without the funds I never had the chance to attend Chloe's wedding and meet her prince charming.

Chloe had fallen in love with her high school sweet-heart—Brody. He was a staunch Canadian and came from an extensive farming heritage. Like his forefathers, he became a farmer, and had taken over his dad's land, where he and Chloe now lived. They had dated off and on all through high school, getting married shortly after prom. Ten years had passed already since they'd tied the knot at eighteen. Everyone assumed she was expecting because they married so quickly, but what people didn't know was Chloe wasn't interested in having children. She secretly hoped for a childless marriage. She hadn't shared her feelings with Brody because she knew he wanted kids. She was sure she could eventually change his mind and provided him with unlimited sex to do so. According to her, he would come to enjoy a carefree sort of life that didn't include children.

Brody was blissfully happy for the first six years of their marriage but had been asking for children for the past four years. He wanted at least four kids, one for each of the four empty bedrooms. He enjoyed watching her take care of the twins and was anxious to make her a mother. Brody loved the sex but was ready for the by-product: a family. Chloe argued with him continually, trying to plead her case. She desperately tried to convince him children would render their sex life nonexistent. Brody would laugh it off, saying she was overreacting. Chloe continued to protest and eventually told Brody she refused to have children. He became very angry and withdrawn, refusing to make love to her unless she was ovulating. He kept track with his very own calendar!

Brody's lack of sex drive, particularly when she couldn't entice him with her erotic cheerleading outfit, affected her deeply. In high school, she'd supported Brody from the sidelines for years with the ensemble. The combination of the uniform and her perfect body made her irresistible; he couldn't keep his hands off her. He adored the short, tight top, showing off her perky breasts and navel. The miniskirt was equally effective, falling just below her firm buttocks to reveal her toned legs. She's kept her enticing outfit all these years and when they fought, she'd slip it on and it would drive him wild— not anymore!

She called frequently, complaining. "He won't even touch me unless I'm ovulating. My outfit had *zero* effect on him!"

She was lonely, convinced he wasn't in love with her anymore, and became suspicious of her husband's intentions toward other women. She figured he was seeing someone else because men just didn't refuse sex! So, the only logical answer, according to Chloe: he was getting it someplace else.

Their relationship wasn't always bad. It was more like a roller coaster. She was happiest between cycles, when she should have been ovulating; Chloe had been deceiving her husband for years, taking injections for birth control. During these moments, Brody showered her with affection and love. When she didn't become pregnant, he became withdrawn, which would upset her all over again. Every month, she was up, then down. He began to suspect she was taking contraceptives. He questioned her. She lied.

There were never going to be any babies. Chloe had always been pushy and determined. She was the same person I had known as a kid; she always got the last piece of watermelon!

If Chloe wanted it, Chloe got it, plain and simple.

Chapter 5
Hello Canada

THE WHEELS TOUCHED DOWN IN HALIFAX AT 5:24 p.m. I could hardly wait to get off the plane, excited to finally see Chloe after all these years. I'd hoped to arrive sooner, wanting to spend as much time with Chloe as possible, but this had been the only available flight. Booking last minute didn't allow for many choices.

For the occasion, I wore my best fitted jeans, which hugged all the right places. I complimented my jeans with an equally fitted Florida Gators t-shirt, Chloe's favorite college football team. The week before, I'd gone shopping for her present, when I noticed the Gators t-shirt. We were roughly the same size; I tried it on, making sure it would fit her properly. I liked it so much I bought one for myself. I was keeping up with our tradition; we'd often bought the same clothing as children. My original plan was to ship it to her but now I was able to deliver it in person.

Once inside the airport, I was able to free myself from the slow-moving group of passengers exiting the plane and anxiously headed for the arrival area, where loved ones were waiting patiently for their wayward travelers. Too impatient to take the escalator, I took the stairs, noticing several men's eyes on my voluminous breasts as they bounced in unison with my quick steps. *Enjoy the show*, I thought, then snickered. *Perhaps they're Florida Gator fans now?*

Several people had flowers in hand and an energetic boy bounced up and down with a welcome home sign he'd obviously made. I scanned the crowd, hoping to catch a glimpse of Chloe in the large crowd. Nothing yet.

Several eyes diverted elsewhere, although some remained on me. I didn't want their attention. I'd perfected my look for Chloe. I ran a hand through my thick hair, teasing out a snarl, then flipped it back over my shoulders, trying to freshen up; I felt a little nervous. Not having seen her since I was thirteen, I was anxious for her to see how I had changed; people always looked different in photos.

I wandered around for the next several minutes, hoping to see Chloe. Still no luck. The luggage carousel squeaked as it started up; I walked over to wait for my suitcase. A couple of months back I had replaced my old black suitcase with an easy-to-spot pink one; since I was making good money I'd planned on travelling more. It was already coming in handy. Another few minutes passed before it came around the bend in the carousel. I lifted it off with ease, having packed lightly for the three-day visit. I returned to the passenger pickup area with all its eager faces waiting for loved ones. The crowd thinned as people embraced one another and headed toward the exit. Still no Chloe.

I nibbled the nail on my pinky, a terrible habit I used to channel nervous energy or concern. *Had I given her the wrong flight time?*

Someone tapped my shoulder and I turned to see her husband, Brody, who I recognized from Chloe's social media photos. Rugged and handsome with deep green eyes and short brown hair, he was the type of guy who deserved a second glance. Without a word, he lifted me into a bear hug. I felt tiny in his thick arms. His embrace was filled with affection and warmth. After about five seconds, he set me back down onto the ground then stepped back and held me at arm's length. "Bree! I'm so happy to finally meet you. What an honor. You're even more stunning in person."

I smiled and blushed, friendliness and shame combining in an awkward mix. I was genuinely happy to meet him, but felt like a hypocrite, knowing the truth about Chloe's deception. I pulled myself together. "Well, I'm as equally pleased to meet you. What a pleasure. I have heard so much about you." I gave him a slight curtsy, trying to be silly to distract his attention away from the emerging redness in my cheeks.

"And I've heard lots about you, my dear. Sorry I'm late. We just had a new addition to the farm, a baby calf. He's been sick, so I was caring from him. That's why I'm delayed."

I could see already he was a good man with a kind soul. He didn't appear to be the cheating monster Chloe had made him out to be. After working at the Chic Chick for so long, I'd become somewhat of a self-proclaimed expert at detecting cheaters.

"Where's Chloe?" I looked around, hoping to see her pop out from behind something or other.

"She's not much of a city driver, as you well know, so she asked me to come get you."

"Is she waiting in the car?"

"No, she's prepping your room and getting ready for your arrival."

"Oh." I hoped he couldn't hear the disappointment in my voice.

If he had, it didn't show. He smiled wide. "Chloe's looking forward to seeing you. She adores you and always has wonderful things to say about you. Let's head out . . . you two can start to catch up." Brody affectionately squeezed my shoulder, making me feel better, grabbed my suitcase with his free hand, and nodded toward the exit.

The drive to Bellevue was about thirty minutes. The highways in Nova Scotia did not allow for the high speeds of New York, so I was able to roll down the window in Brody's old truck, tie up my hair in a loose bun to avoid any tangles, and enjoy the warm breeze on my face. I closed my eyes while I breathed in the fresh air. Brody, silent, let me enjoy the moment. After several minutes of filling my lungs with the country air, I inquired, "So, Chloe tells me you love to farm. Please tell me more."

He raised his eyebrows, as if asking, "Do you really want to know?" I nodded. He drew in a breath, ready to tell his story. "I've always wanted to take over my dad's farm, ever since I graduated from high school." Brody flicked a bug off the dash which the open window had invited in.

"He's worked very hard all his life and is growing older, and I love the work and want to help. It just made sense to carry on the tradition. He and Mom still work on the farm but for the most part, they've retired and live in town. He's a man to be admired: strong, honest, and hardworking. He's been a good husband and a great father . . . old stock and proud of it. I can only strive to be the kind of person he represents." Brody straightened his back, looking ready for the challenge.

"Well, from what Chloe's told me and from the brief time I've known you, I think you already fit all your father's traits and more." I wasn't lying, she did adore him . . . when he paid attention to her.

Now it was his turn to blush. He smiled but then his face turned gloomy. "Except the father part," he whispered under his breath. His shoulders slumped, and his eyes held a sadness I knew all too well. Brody's childless marriage had caused him the same depth of melancholy I had been feeling off and on over the past year.

Young and naïve, at twenty-five I had fallen in love with a married man, Adam, seven years my senior. His company provided restaurant supplies to the Chic Chick. At the time I had been working at the club for a year and the owner liked and trusted me, giving me extra responsibilities, which included calling Adam. We were business associates at first but everything changed after we'd met at a conference. We were together for almost two years before he broke my heart.

That was a year ago, but most days the pain was still acute, like it had only happened yesterday. Now, I could see the same hollowness and emptiness in Brody's eyes. The sadness was almost tangible. Nothing I could say would comfort him because Chloe wouldn't give him the only thing that could: a baby.

I was upset with Chloe for stringing him along. I barely knew him, but anyone could see he was a good person who deserved a family. Chloe would have to talk about it as soon as we were alone.

Not knowing what to say, I reached over and turned on the radio. Not surprisingly, it was set to a country station. A man's voice filled the air, singing a sad song about his lover who had left him for another. I understood the country singer's sadness, as I understood Brody's, because we were all in the same boat.

The only thing that had somewhat diminished my pain was time. There was no magic pill to expedite the healing. I knew, because I'd tried to find it, wanting to numb the ache. My previous one-night stands and drinking had only been temporary solutions to my problems.

We drove the rest of the way in silence, letting the radio do the talking. Both deep in our own thoughts, preoccupied by our troubles, we seemed to understand each other without saying a word. Fifteen minutes later, we arrived at the farm house. As we drove up the gravel driveway, Chloe came running out of the house. She was beaming and emitted an infectious radiance. Any grudge I'd been holding against her for not coming to the airport suddenly dissipated. As she got closer to the truck, her short flowing sun dress danced in the breeze. By the looks of it, she had nothing underneath. That was my Chloe, free as a bird; always the life of the party. A surprise she settled down right out of high school.

She and Brody had dated throughout high school, but they'd broken up a handful of times. The breakups were always temporary, three or four weeks max. Chloe would dump him for some ridiculous reason or another. She liked drama. Then she'd take the opportunity to sleep with other men. According to her, it wasn't considered cheating because they were on a break. Her conscience was free. I don't think Brody would have seen it that way, but he never found out, so it hadn't become an issue.

Chloe couldn't live without male attention even when on a short-term break up, so I suspect that's why she married so young. She always needed the security of a man to take care of her and Brody gave her that.

"Bree!" Despite her small frame she grabbed me in a big bear hug, equally as affectionate as her husband's had been. I was roughly the same size as Chloe, only taller, but we looked completely different. She was a Barbie doll with lots of makeup, manicured nails, and perfect hair.

I often wore very little makeup or none. I liked sports, the outdoors, and had a natural beauty—not the done-up kind like Chloe. Even our personalities were different. She emitted a *come talk to me* attitude. She loved men's attention and sought it out. I, on the other hand, preferred to stay low key, out of the limelight . . . and out of reach of their wandering hands.

She released me and stepped back. "Let me see you." She took a long look up and down, nodding her head in approval. "You're beautiful, Bree. Absolutely stunning. I like your Gators shirt. Great taste." She winked and gave two thumbs up.

"I'm glad you approve! I put in an extra effort just for you."

"Aren't you sweet." She took my arm and turned me towards the house. "We have so much to talk about," she squealed in delight before pulling me toward the front doors of the farmhouse.

"Well, on that note," Brody was grinning at us and shaking his head, looking amused and pleased to see his wife so happy, "I'll be heading back to the barn to check in on the new calf."

"Yes dear, sounds like a wonderful idea." It was clear Chloe didn't want him around, but smiled at him sweetly, as if she didn't want to hurt his feelings. "We have lots of girl talk to catch up on . . . no boys allowed." She winked again, this time at her husband. "I'll make some fresh lemonade with the bag of lemons your mom brought by today. Come back to the house in a couple hours after we've had some time to catch up."

She blew him a kiss and he played along, reaching above his head, pretending to catch the imaginary gift with his hand. He stuffed it in his pocket. "I'll keep this one for later."

Brody jumped in his truck and sped off, spitting gravel as he fishtailed along the driveway. It appeared his wife's imaginary kiss had added extra fuel to his day.

If I'd been an innocent bystander, I would've thought they were happy. I looked over at Chloe expecting to see the same happiness on her face, but tears formed in the corners of her eyes. As Brody drove farther out of sight, the tears streamed down her face. I put my arm around her shoulders and guided her to the porch swing, which I knew Brody had bought for her shortly after they'd moved in.

This was going to be our first time sitting together on a swing without a smile.

Chapter 6
Rock-A-Bye

THE SWING LOOKED AND FELT FAMILIAR: SOFT cushions, a wide seat, and bright white paint. Chloe had enjoyed my family's swing as a child and now had one for herself, but it wasn't as I remembered. Life's realities had replaced our blissful, carefree childhood.

She slumped backward into the seat, weeping as she mumbled something incomprehensible about Brody and a baby. She put her head on my lap and started to sob uncontrollably. The scent of rosemary mint shampoo filled the air as I brushed away strands of auburn hair from her face.

I lightly pushed my feet against the wooden floor boards. We started moving back and forth, ever so slowly. We held a similar silence to one I'd shared with Brody on the drive home from the airport. I let her cry until there were no tears left, providing her with comfort and companionship while we rocked back and forth. After ten minutes, she fell asleep on my lap, emotionally exhausted.

I consoled her with my presence as she slept. Through her tears and red, runny nose, Chloe was beautiful. She had small, delicate features and flawless skin. *Perhaps being beautiful was a curse*? I thought.

Would Brody love her without her beauty? Or if she were blind or scarred? Did he tolerate her non-traditional ways because she was easy on the eyes? How could he continue to stay with her when he suspected she was deceiving him? Would he still love her if he knew the truth?

I'd read once that good-looking people were treated better and had easier lives but sometimes I didn't believe this was true. Beauty could be a curse too! I had experienced the positive benefit firsthand when I'd got the job at the Chic Chick. Being beautiful had helped but I'd never allowed myself to rely solely on my looks. Having a personality was key—I knew my appeal wouldn't last forever.

For Chloe, her looks were a bargaining tool she used to manipulate and control people. A curse in this instance, I'd say! During high school, she'd bragged in her letters to me that she never had to study or do any homework because she had a handful of classmates to do her bidding. However, she eventually suffered when she went to college, hoping to avoid having babies. She'd lasted one semester before dropping out because of extremely low grades. Let me correct myself. She did get one good grade in college. She was *friendly* with her business professor. I never dared ask how she managed to pull off an A+ in his class…

I ran the back of my hand over her cheek, love swelled in my heart. I loved her inspite of her faults, and she loved me despite mine. We were fortunate to have each other.

I shifted in the swing, legs numb from being in the same position for almost an hour. My movement woke Chloe.

She sat up swiftly and reached her slender arms above her head to stretch. As she lowered them, she ran her fingers through her hair like a brush, trying to take out the knots that had formed while she slept. She turned and smiled, her voice steady again. "Whew! I finally got it out of my system. Thanks, Bree." She leaned over and hugged me.

"Do you want to talk about it?" I probed.

"Nope. We aren't wasting any more time on my tears. Let's get ready to party." Her tone and attitude had changed drastically. I didn't want to pursue the issue, so I let it drop.

"I can't argue with that! I came dressed and ready to party."

She looked at my clothes, then at my face. "Oh no you don't, Bree. You could use a little more makeup for the evening." She wrinkled her nose at me disapprovingly, knowing full well I would not take offence.

It was a running joke between us, I didn't wear enough face paint for her liking. I laughed. Being beautiful was a pre-requisite for any of Chloe's friends and I was no exception. "Sure, I'll put on a little more blush just for you."

"Amen! I was worried we'd have to stay in."

She snickered, back to her usual self. She showed no signs of being troubled, but I knew her make-believe life was causing her pain again.

"Let's hurry and head out before my hubby gets back or he'll want to tag along."

"But Chloe you were supposed to have lemonade made for him when he got back," I protested.

"I changed my mind. He can make his own lemonade. Besides, he'll eventually show up at the pub anyhow. He's always checking up on me." She sighed. "Sometimes my only escape is the ladies' room!"

"Well, you're lucky to have a man who loves you so much," I insisted, encouraging her to show some love for her husband.

She shrugged, tipped her head to the side, placing both hands on top of each other, under her chin, using them like a pedestal, and batted her long eyelashes. "Of course. What's not to love about this face?"

I rolled my eyes. She hopped off the swing, but I didn't budge, glaring at her while shaking my head. "We should wait for him."

"No," she said simply and grabbed my hand, pulling me to my feet. "It's dancing time."

I debated resisting her efforts further, wanting to wait for Brody, but as she tugged me along, I decided it was 'her' birthday after all and there was no point in arguing.

We ran into the house like children being chased by an imaginary boogey man. We were laughing again, just like we'd done when we were young.

Chapter 7
Say Cheese!

"FIRST ONE TO THE TOP OF THE STAIRS BUYS THE first round of drinks," Chloe announced as she pushed past me. We ran up the stairs, fighting for first place.

I managed to take the lead but tripped on the last step and fell, twisting my left ankle. I hit the floor, letting out a yelp and moaned, "It wasn't graceful at all, but I win." I tried to stand up, not getting far. My ankle ached.

Chloe was already heading back down the stairs. "I'm getting some ice. We have way too much dancing ahead of us to have you injured. The locals have limited moves and I was hoping a classic New Yorker like yourself could show them a thing or two on the dance floor."

I called after her, "Obviously you haven't seen me dance lately! I can't even make it up the stairs without falling!"

She returned almost immediately with an ice pack and handed it to me.

"But don't you worry about me. I'll be fine. I didn't come all this way to just sit on a bar stool and let you have all the fun." But as the words left my mouth, the throbbing in my ankle intensified; I grimaced. Rolling back the cuff of my jeans, I placed the cold ice pack on my injury. The throbbing subsided . . . slightly.

Chloe helped me to the bathroom, tucking me in close, but stopped in the doorway, frowning. "He left the lid up on the toilet seat again," she complained. "Married life isn't what I'd hoped. I seem to do all the work around here." She placed a hand on her slim hip shaking her head side to side, her reddish curls lightly brushing against my face as she showed her displeasure.

The bathroom didn't look very tidy, but it appeared to be mostly her stuff cluttering the room. Chloe hadn't worked a day since she married Brody. She was his princess and he kept her well. Chloe had announced early in their marriage she was allergic to cleaning solutions, so they had a cleaner come every week. She rarely cooked but she did self-proclaim to be the best lemonade maker in all of Bellevue.

I'd just arrived and my visit would be short, so I felt it was best not to refute her claim of being overworked. As for the lemonade, that was left to be determined. Maybe she'd put her mother-in-law's lemons to good use the next afternoon. Besides, I knew Chloe well enough to realize she had her own sense of reality and didn't take well to advice from others.

She propped me against the wall for support and closed the toilet seat, providing a place to sit. Careful not to bump my ankle, I eased into place. Laying the ice pack over the affected area once again, I winced in pain. Chloe had a look of pity then her eyes brightened. She put a finger up in the air. "Wait, I have another solution. Something better than ice."

Chloe headed down the stairs a second time. I watched through the open bathroom door as, unlike myself, she gracefully descended the stairs. Within moments she was back up with four frosted beer bottles. She handed over two of them. "I got them from the beer fridge in the basement. The one I told you about. They are super cold. Alcohol will definitely take the edge off."

She often mentioned the popularity of their near-freezing beers among their family and friends. I twisted off the cap, tossed it in the trash bin, and took a long drink. The cold liquid traveled down my throat and I felt an almost-immediate cooling sensation in my chest. It was excellent. No wonder their beer fridge was so popular!

I removed the ice pack, replacing it with the beer bottle, rolling it over my ankle. My skin tingled. "Well, so much for my shaved legs! This bottle's so cold it gave me goose bumps. I'm going to have to shave again," I grumbled.

"With the size of those jugs," she lifted an eyebrow and gestured to my chest, "the guys around here won't care." Chloe's thoughts often circled around sex and she liked to talk dirty. Not that I wasn't guilty of it too, but I only used it as a playful tool while making love, not in everyday conversation.

"I've told you before, I'm done with men for another five years at least." I crossed my arms over my chest to prove the point.

Chloe rolled her eyes and sighed. "Your loss, hun. You're single and delicious. You need to let go of that Adam guy.

He was such a jerk anyhow. He broke you in two. He was never going to leave his—" She stopped, seeing my back stiffen. She knew better than to mention his name.

I glared at her. "You know I don't like to talk about *him*."

Adam was a sensitive subject. I'd dated a married man and wasn't proud of it, but I was deeply in love with him, so I stayed. Then karma found me! He cheated on me with another women . . . another mistress. The betrayal left me barren inside, a raw steak cooked blue. I had no interest in a relationship, but somewhere deep down I still hoped love would find me.... when I was ready.

"I can see! Relax. I'm just trying to help. You need to loosen up and get yourself out there. They say the best way to get over someone is to get under someone." She gave me a sexy little wink and pushed her tongue against the inside of her right cheek, the symbolic gesture for a blow job.

I shook my head in protest. "No thanks. Let's agree, no more talking about *him*."

"Fine by me." She reached under the sink and took out a large basket overflowing with makeup and hair supplies. "Well, if you don't want to get lucky tonight, you're at least going to look like you want to. You're my captive now," she declared, trying to sound like a pirate. "You're stuck on that seat whether you like it or not, little lass. I'll make ye walk the plank if ye resist." A makeup brush was already in my face, wielded like a sword.

I started to protest.

Chloe put her make-believe sword to my lips. "I know, I know. You don't like to wear makeup and when you do, it's not a lot. Obviously." She raised an eyebrow and wrinkled her nose, like she had before on the swing. She kept the brush to my lips, so I couldn't respond. "You're in my house, so you will do as I like."

While I was held 'captive', she preached about the benefits of makeup as she added rose blush along my cheek bones and additional eye shadow to my lids.

"OK, why did I come here to visit? Oh yes, to be tortured and bossed around by the likes of you." I stuck out my tongue and crossed my eyes. "Just like you do to your husband."

The lightness in her mood suddenly turned dark. I'd unknowingly hit a nerve.

Her eyes narrowed. "What are you talking about?"

"It's just… you two seem so happy together. Why don't you want children?" I couldn't keep the touch of judgment out of my words.

"I don't want to ruin *my* birthday. I'm not talking about *it*." She had a look I knew too well: *drop it before I have a fit.* She returned the tongue and crossed-eyes, likely hoping to defuse the situation.

When we were twelve, we'd started a tradition: crossing our eyes and sticking our tongues out at each other after we fought. It was our own unique way of saying "I'm sorry." It had started when we'd fought over something silly . . . She liked a boy and he liked me. Naturally, Chloe being Chloe, she was upset with me. The argument had lasted for two weeks until, surprisingly, she reached out to me.

* * *

It was Monday and the big yellow school bus had just deposited me at the end of the driveway. The red flag on our large steel mailbox was up, indicating the mailman had placed some goodies inside. One of my responsibilities after school was bringing the mail home.

I yanked open the mailbox and cautiously peered inside. The neighbor boy, from two farmhouses down, would sometimes put worms in the mailbox to scare me. It had only happened twice but I refused to put my hand in before doing a thorough check. I couldn't see any creepy crawlers, but I did see a beautiful purple envelope waiting for me to claim it. I reached inside and pulled it out. My name was written in block letters on the front. I recognized Chloe's writing. I ran my finger along the inner edge and opened it. Inside was a small piece of paper:

5:30 BY THE STOP SIGN

I was elated to finally hear from her. Chloe had been miserable at school and wouldn't even look my way despite my attempts to negotiate a peace talk. It looked like she was finally ready to make amends. The only stop sign in the area was near her place, the farmhouse to the south.

I ran home, up the stairs, and straight into my bedroom. The princess clock on my bedside table read 4:45. I took a quick shower and put on some fresh clothes. I also cleaned up my room, in case she wanted to come over to play after we made up. It was 5:25 when I left the room. Rushing through the front door, I yelled out to Mom, "I'm going to see Chloe."

"Lovely, honey," she said, her voice happy. "I'm so glad you two are talking again."

I had been harassing Mom daily to play with me since I had no Chloe around to fill my time. She'd be just as happy as me to have Chloe back. I ran all the way to the stop sign, about four minutes from my front steps.

Chloe was leaning against the sign's wooden pole. The large stop sign hung above her head, making her look smaller than she was. She looked up at the sound of my shoes kicking up the gravel and started running toward me. We stopped just short of each other and embraced into a whole-hearted hug.

She didn't seem to want to let me go and I felt so loved and missed, all at once. Chloe held onto me for several minutes before finally stepping back. She looked down and lightly kicked the gravel, as if she didn't know what to say. I giggled, and she looked up. I crossed my eyes and stuck out my tongue. We both began to laugh. It was like our argument had never happened.

Then we did what we always did on Monday nights, swam in my dad's dugout. Dad had turned the previous owner's livestock watering hole into our very own "swimming pool." As a child, he'd swum in dugouts, creating fond memories, and had wanted to offer the same opportunity to his only daughter. He managed to convince Mom it was "OK". Her only stipulation: Dad treat the water and I close my eyes—a precaution; Dad's water treatment plan was always a work in progress.

Chloe and I swam until the sun began to set. We didn't hash out the reasons we'd fought. Instead, we took the time to catch up. From then on, we rarely used words to settle our disagreements, just silly faces.

* * *

Chloe had finished plastering my face with makeup, so she turned her talents onto herself. She was skillful with her "sword" from years of practice.

I sipped my second beer as she worked her magic. "Say cheese," I requested, holding up my phone. She turned, flashing a pearly white smile. I snapped a photo of her, makeup brush in hand. A true reflection of Chloe. As I waited for my little princess to finish, I admired the photo and a soft pang of emotion welled up in my throat. I loved her like a sister. I updated her profile photo on my phone with the one I'd just taken. The photo of us eating watermelon as children replaced by Chloe, all grown up.

Miraculously, the throbbing in my foot subsided. Chloe was right: the alcohol was assisting with the healing process. It was time to dance.

As I sipped my third ice cold beer, I thought, *Maybe, just maybe, I'll take Chloe's advice after all and get myself under someone.*

Chapter 8
Three's a Crowd

WE PULLED UP TO THE LOCAL TAVERN IN CHLOE'S brand-new white Jeep Wrangler. Brody had surprised her a month prior with a shopping trip to the local car dealership. An early birthday present, it was a nice ride compared to his old truck.

The Local Tavern hadn't changed a bit since our parents would sneak away for a couple of pints after we were tucked in bed. Dozens of antique signs still hung outside, giving the bar a welcoming appeal. They'd been clinging to the old building so long they were molded into the wood, permanent fixtures, just as the tavern had become a permanent watering hole for the locals. The only sign with a recent coat of paint stood posted above the front doors, "Local Tavern." Hand-created by an amateur, it suited the Tavern's decor and seemed to invite people inside with its subtle description.

Chloe put her new ride in park and hastily exited the driver's side door. She was bouncing toward the front steps before I'd even had a chance to step out of the Jeep. She'd chosen a sexy country outfit, complete with short denim skirt, to celebrate her birthday. The snug-fitting tank top showed off her breasts, the spaghetti straps looking even thinner under their strain. She'd finished off the look with some short red cowboy boots and had tied her auburn hair in a ponytail.

She was glowing with anticipation, anxious to be adored. Judging from the sound of male voices hollering inside, she was in luck.

She swung the front door open widely, alerting everyone to her arrival. The voices became even louder, hooting and hollering filling the night air. They were happy to see her and she them.

I positioned myself just inside the doorway to avoid the attention and inconspicuously watched as she twirled around in a full circle and curtsied, showing off her assets as she did. A couple of men at the bar waved her over, but it was clear she had her sights set on someone else.

Chloe beelined for a striking man about our age leaning up against the pool table. His eyes focused on her attributes as she ran over. She threw her arms around his neck and pushed herself into him. He leaned in and kissed her neck ever so lightly before moving away. With the attention on Chloe, I knew it was a good time to work my way into the tavern. I made my way over to the pool table and stood off to the side while she poured herself all over her friend.

"Come on now, sexy. You know I can't resist those hugs." The lust on his face was unmistakable.

"It's my birthday! You can't deny a birthday girl her birthday wishes." Chloe's eyes were a little too mischievous and her body was hanging a little too close for anyone not

43

to suspect they were aching for each other despite the ring of her finger. Chloe whispered something into his ear and he grinned wolfishly.

I had to admit he was a very fine specimen, but she was married. He didn't have a ring on his finger, so the situation was only problematic from her side of the equation.

His dark brown eyes sparkled as Chloe continued to whisper into his ear and press her breasts against his forearm. He was built like a football player. His brown hair was tousled, shaggy, and sexy and the sun had done a wonderful job of tanning his skin to a golden brown. I could see why Chloe was attracted to him.

He was so perfect he reminded me of a cupcake I'd purchased the week before. I had been drawn into a fancy bakery by the display of impeccable cupcakes in the window. It was evident the baker had taken a lot of time sculpting his cupcakes into masterpieces. They were pricey, but I bought one anyhow. I admired it for a few minutes before I bit into it, expecting the inside to taste as perfect as the outside looked. Instead, I was disappointed by a dry, stale cupcake. I wondered if this perfect-looking man was inwardly stale, like my cupcake, or if he was a good man like Brody.

Chloe finally turned around, taking notice of me. She smiled and pulled me into what little space was left between her and cupcake man.

"This is my very best friend, Bree! She's from New York and has traveled a long way to celebrate my birthday with me. Isn't she sweet, Caleb?"

I secretly bestowed him the nickname *Caleb the cupcake* and snickered to myself, amused. Caleb the cupcake looked just as pleased with me as he did Chloe. He slipped his arms around both of our waists and drew us into his chest. It was even firmer than it looked. Caleb smiled like a cat who had just eaten a canary and uttered, in a deep sexy voice, "You bet she's sweet. Now I know what I want for *my* birthday: the *two* of you!"

Chloe slapped his chest, disappointed by his comment. He laughed, unconcerned, and pulled us both closer. He tilted his head forward, placing it between our bosoms, and licked his lips. I started to back away, but Caleb the cupcake placed his hand on my backside and steered me back into his chest. I wasn't interested in his attention. Chloe could have him. As far as I was concerned, he *was* like my stale cupcake: all looks, but tasteless.

I turned to break from his grip, and that's when I saw Brody heading toward us, looking as mad as a hornet who'd just been swatted away from its food. I hadn't seen him come in, but Brody had sure seen us. Caleb, just lifting his head from admiring Chloe's breasts, was taken by surprise when Brody's fist connected with his perfect nose. Crack!

I backed away quickly. I'd seen a few fights at the Chic Chick and knew when to disperse. Caleb's blood splattered Chloe's white tank top, speckling it bright red. She stood still, in shock, not moving. Caleb stumbled forward, falling to his knees, accidentally knocking Chloe into the side of the pool table. A pool cue, improperly stored, connected with her back and she shrieked in pain.

The anger in Brody's eyes erased immediately and he rushed to help is wife—she refused. Chloe was sobbing at this point, although I suspected it was more from embarrassment than pain. "Back off, Brody! I've told you before—Caleb and I are just friends."

Brody opened his mouth to protest but before he could say anything, Chloe's hand was across his face. Now it was his turn to look shocked.

Chloe was so mad she was trembling. The tears had stopped, replaced with fury. She reached over, grabbed Caleb's hand, and pulled him to his feet. His hands were covered in blood and his nose was still dripping red.

"I'm going to make this up to you, Caleb." She affirmed, leaning into him. Caleb stepped behind her, looking happy to have some distance from Brody. Everyone could see Chloe was in control now and was teaching her husband a lesson. She was purposefully embarrassing him, as he had done to her. "Brody, if you follow us out of this bar, I'm leaving you. Do you understand?"

Brody hung his head in defeat and nodded. Chloe wrapped her arm around Caleb's trim waist and pulled him into her side, supporting his unstable legs. She was clearly, but unfairly, taking Caleb's side.

The music had stopped, and everyone was watching the love triangle's drama unfold while they sipped their beers. Some looked amused, some horrified, and others indifferent. They parted, making a path as Caleb and Chloe moved toward the front doors. As they passed the bar, Chloe rang the old cow bell hanging on the wall. "Hey, bartender! Next round is on my husband for interrupting the party." The whole bar began to holler and whistle at the good news. The bartender looked pleased: the more people drank, the more they tipped, and it looked to be the start of a very prosperous night.

I turned to Brody, who was standing where Chloe had left him, his eyes fixed on the doorway, as if contemplating his next move. He didn't appear to be embarrassed by the spectacle nor did he seem concerned about the round of drinks that was going to cost him a few days' pay. It seemed all he cared about was his wife leaving the bar with her arm around Caleb.

A wave of pity washed over me, I had an overwhelming desire to help him. I gently guided him over to an empty table and we sat down. I motioned a server our way and ordered two beers.

We sat in silence waiting for her return. While searching for words, I picked at the table, noticing the previous occupants had spilled their beverages, leaving sticky pools all over the wooden surface. Within minutes she magically appeared from the crowd, two bottles in hand. About to ask for assistance with the sticky mess, I noted a towel stuffed in her discolored and stained apron. Her cloth was just as dirty. I let it go.

I gingerly pushed both bottles over to Brody. "Here, start with these," my voice cheerful and encouraging. He needed liquid medicine ASAP.

He reached over and took the first beer. He finished it in one reckless gulp. The beer bottle looked tiny in his broad, well-textured hand from years of working on the farm. Although his hands looked coarse, I was sure he had a gentle touch. They suited his tall frame and lean build. Chloe didn't realize how good she had it with this man. He clearly loved her and would do anything for her, except agreeing to have a childless marriage.

He seemed to be deep in thought as he reached for the second beer but was still kind enough to offer it to me first. I declined. He tipped the second beer back and consumed it like the first, in one gulp. He wiped his lips, ready to talk. "I love her so much and the thought of her being with someone else drives me insane. I know she's not the cheating type and she loves me too much to be unfaithful, but I still get jealous."

He looked downward like a beaten dog. He needed to be more cat-like: they don't give their love so freely, it needs to be earned. This guy deserved better.

"Well, you can either grab another drink or go chasing after Chloe, but remember she specifically asked you not to." In case he was going to choose the latter despite my warning I cautioned, "A word of advice before you run after Chloe: there is no use chasing something that doesn't want to be caught."

He lifted his head, his dark green eyes filling with fear. I suspected it was the fear that maybe Chloe didn't want him after all—the same fear I'd felt after I'd lost Adam. His lip quivered, and his puppy dog eyes drooped to another level. I didn't think it was possible for him to look any more forlorn, but he did. *Is this what I looked like when Adam no longer wanted me?* Heartbreak was ugly, and it was difficult to see someone of his stature reduced to rubble.

Before he had the chance to tear up and embarrass himself further, I tapped him lightly on the cheek, trying to get his attention and distract him. It was the same cheek

Chloe had slapped earlier, still slightly red from her assault. He looked up, surprised.

"I thought farm boys were tough." I got up, raised both my hands into fists, lightly boxing his well-toned abs. Without a doubt, a firm six pack was concealed underneath his checkered shirt.

He gave a forced grin. I was making headway, so I monopolized the opportunity to change his mind and poked at his sides. He was very ticklish and started to laugh. It was contagious.

Our laughter grabbed the attention of a waitress who was passing by with a tray of free shooters, paid for by Brody, thanks to his lovely wife. I grabbed four shooters from the tray and handed him three. I raised my glass above my head and he followed suit. "Here's to wishing for a better night," I chuckled, hoping he'd do the same. I clinked his glass. He shrugged. It was a start.

We finished our shooters within minutes. I motioned the overwhelmed waitress over, wanting access to her tray, yet again, before all the precious liquid disappeared. I lightened her load, commandeering the tray. She protested, I raised my hand, stopping her complaints. "Hey, he's buying and I'm tipping! So, expect a pleasant surprise at the end of the night."

She rolled her eyes. "Fine by me, hun. I just need the tray. They're hard to come by in this joint and I have more drinks to serve. Ever since his wife rang that damn bell I've been run off my feet." An older lady, who appeared to have been working at the tavern since it opened, she had little patience for the likes of me and I couldn't blame her.

I knew better than to touch her tray, but Brody was paying, so a little extra customer service was expected as far as I was concerned.

"No problem, ma'am." I placed the last of the drinks on our table, removed my hand from her precious tray, and released her back into the wilds of the bar. She hustled away, her bleach-blonde hair a stark contrast among the dark figures. It was helpful, making her easy to spot—a beacon in the dark. And such a quality was important for anyone looking for a drink.

I counted six plastic mini cups, enough to keep us busy for the next little while. The only temporary therapy I knew that worked one hundred percent of the time on a wounded heart was alcohol . . . or impromptu sex. Brody was faithful and I wasn't about to sleep with my best friend's husband, so that left getting Brody drunk. He could forget all his worries, at least for a while.

"So, what do you say? A round of pool or dancing?" I made sure chasing Chloe wasn't among my options.

He tossed back three of the six shooters before deciding. Grabbing me by the elbow, he steered me toward the dance floor.

Chapter 9
"You sunk my battleship!"

SITTING AT THE BAR, ENJOYING A BREAK FROM THE dance floor, I took the time to take in the decor. The Tavern encompassed the complete country western experience: Southern charm, homestyle cooking, line dancing, and last but not least, mechanical bull riding—although no one had tried the bull. A large, handwritten sign hung around its neck, which read, "OUT OF ORDER. Sorry folks." A red-lipped kiss—maybe Blondie's—marked the bottom of the note.

My phone vibrated in my pocket. A missed call from Chloe. I hadn't even thought of her until then. Fortunately, Brody was line dancing with some of his buddies. He loved to dance and knew everyone in the bar. People seemed to gravitate to him. He was well-liked. It was no surprise.

I headed to the bathroom in search of privacy in case Brody came stumbling over to drag me onto the dance floor. I didn't want him to have any reminders of his wife; it would set him back into puppy mode again. I was still hopeful he would learn to be more like a cat!

As the bathroom door swung shut, I looked over my shoulder, pleased to see the cute blonde with the sparsely freckled face steering him toward the pool table. He'd introduced her as Emma, his best friend's kid sister. They'd played a couple of games earlier, and although competitive, she'd lost both times. I was sure she figured all the whiskey in his system had diminished his skills enough she could claim a victory.

I was feeling under the influence myself. The alcohol I'd ingested to fuel my evening was taking control of my body. My bladder was signaling it needed relief, even before Chloe called. I stepped over the toilet paper littering the floor and tried to find the cleanest stall available; my choices were limited.

Washing my hands, I looked around for a place to sit. If I was going to tackle a conversation with Chloe, I needed to get off my feet —I foreshadowed lots of whining. Although I was annoyed with her, it was none of my business what went on in their marriage. I really didn't want to take sides, just help Brody feel better.

The counter beside the sink seemed the best choice, so I hopped up and sat down. The previous occupants had left little puddles of water, fumbling to turn off the taps in their drunken state and I unknowingly sat in their mess. As my jeans soaked up the water, I dialed Chloe's number, shaking my head and mumbling to myself, "Oh, great! My ass is wet!"

Chloe picked up mid-ring, catching the tail end of my last words. "You want to screw the vet?" she snickered. "You met Trevor? He's a great catch, the local vet. Plus, he's *rich*."

"No. My butt is wet. I didn't say anything about a vet! Although, come to think of it . . ." I laughed, jokingly growling into the phone. "How can I find this Trevor guy?"

"He lives just down the road from the bar. Want me to hook you up? I have his number."

Trevor's name was volunteered with a little too much affection and her ability to call him so easily, at such a late hour, led me to assume Trevor might be another one of her 'friends,' like Caleb the cupcake. I scolded myself for being so judgmental, but I couldn't help the thoughts being forced into my head. I knew he wasn't on her speed dial to provide medical services to the farm animals. She hadn't stepped foot inside a barn since Brody put a ring on her finger.

Before they were married, she had gone to the barn a few times, only to fool around with Brody in the hay loft. His parents never allowed any funny business in the house. It wasn't fair to judge Chloe, but obviously, I had inadvertently taken sides.

"I'm sure you do," I hissed into the phone. I surprised myself at how protective I was of Brody. We had bonded over the previous hours and I had come a little too quickly to his defence.

"Are you accusing me of *something*? *Really?* Who are you to judge? You were having sex with a *married* man for years and now it looks like you want my husband too," she hissed back.

Her words cut deep. She knew I had residual guilt. I had tried to break off the affair, but his assurances were convincing; he was going to leave his wife. According to him, they were "technically" separated. I was livid. Chloe was playing dirty. "He said he was going through a separation and I was stupid enough to believe it. I admit it, but as for *your* husband, he's just that: *your* husband. And I respect that. I don't cheat as carefree as *some* people."

She gasped. We were playing a game of battleship; our words missiles, firing back and forth. I'd injured her; she was readying for retaliation. Not giving her the chance, I continued the attack.

"He's a good man and I know you're a cheater. You were cheating on him even before you were married." I was intoxicated, bold from the grip alcohol had given me and the accusations flowed easily for my lips.

She could see I wasn't about to let up; her ship was quickly sinking. She sighed and changed her approach, relenting a *little*. "Well, I was going to lie . . . but I'm tired of hiding. Of course I'm cheating on him. Didn't you see Caleb? He's gorgeous and pounds me like a machine. Good and hard, just the way I like it." She didn't skip a beat, the verbal judo continuing, happy to finally speak openly about her secrets. "At least Caleb makes love to me. Brody only wants sex to procreate and it's boring as hell. I'll never have *his* babies. Never! I want out of my marriage. I don't love him anymore. I want to be with Caleb!" She inhaled, taking in oxygen, needing more ammunition to carry on. "If I leave, I'll look like the bad person and I'm not! Everyone thinks he's the prefect husband...not this time. He's not coming away from this looking like a saint. This marriage has always been about what he wants, and I don't want any brats." She then let out a small cry and whimper, changing her tune on a dime. "I'm so unhappy, Bree."

I couldn't pity her like I had so many times before; she was trying to blow out Brody's candle, making hers shine brighter. Not anymore!

"Why did you get married then?" I kept my tone even. Chloe instantly stopped crying when I showed no sympathy. I was coming to realize she was very good at manipulating people, including me.

"Because I'm a princess, Bree," she said, matter of factly. "I never wanted to get a job and I knew Brody would provide for me. I thought I'd be able to change his mind about children but he's never going to give it up." She paused before hitting me with the next blow. "I've already figured out my exit plan and I'm willing to be fair about it too. I'd only take *some* of his money, enough to get a house in town. Caleb will take care of the rest."

I shook my head, wondering if I really knew Chloe at all. She was as shallow as she was beautiful. I didn't think she could stoop any lower until I heard the next words out of her mouth...

Chapter 10
What Are Best Friends For?

"WILL YOU SLEEP WITH MY HUSBAND?"

I gasped. Her words took me by surprise. *She must be joking! She's just trying to push my buttons! Even if she doesn't love Brody, surely she doesn't want me sleeping with him. Would she?* "Sure, I'll get right on it," I answered sarcastically, then chortled.

"I'm serious, Bree. Will you sleep with my husband? I know it's a big favor to ask, but just this once . . .?"

She cut me to the core; I suddenly felt sober. Disgust bubbled up inside me, stirring in the depths of my belly, working its way up and searing my throat. My cheeks flushed and my hands shook. I tried to control the impulsive anger emanating from her insane request. Sarcasm eeked in my response. "And why would *my dearest* and *best friend* want me to sleep with *her* husband?"

"Because if he sleeps with you, he'd be the bad guy, not me. No one could blame me for breaking his heart. I'm thinking the best time would be tonight. You two seem to have really hit it off. I know he's drunk because a friend of mine is keeping tabs on him. She's at the bar. He only dances when he's drunk. So, if you sleep—"

Interrupting her, completely pissed by her request, I kept my voice as calm as I could. "Then why don't you ask your friend to do it?"

I couldn't believe it, she was asking me to sleep with her husband as if it were a simple favor, like borrowing a cup of sugar for her lemonade. She expressed no signs of hesitation or remorse. She'd made her decision and was actively setting her plan in motion.

"I know she'd do it, but I don't trust her enough. She'd talk. The whole town would know by tomorrow night. No one can know it's a setup, *no one*. Besides, I think it'd take someone like you, with a big heart and shoulder to cry on, to make him cave. Plus, he's drunk, so that will work in our favor."

Our favor? What? Like we're a team now! Plotting like a bunch of misfits. The nerve of her! My blood was boiling. I was insulted she'd even ask such a thing. Taking my phone I held it out, the screen showing Chloe's smiling face from only a few hours earlier. Oh how things had changed in such a short time! I yelled at the screen, "Just because you're a tramp, what makes you think I am?"

I pressed down so hard on the end icon I thought it would crack under the pressure. Hopping down from the bathroom counter, I headed straight for the bar and ordered two shooters. After tossing them back to back, I sunk to a stool in dismay and replayed the conversation with Chloe. I ordered another drink while my brain frantically tried to figure out what had just happened. *How could she ask this of me? How could she do this to Brody? What would make her even think of doing such a thing?*

It came to me. The light bulb went on, illuminating my senses. Had she suddenly come up with the idea, or had she been planning it for some time? At that moment, I realized she was playing chess and I was her pawn. I surmised she'd planned my visit to Canada for the sole purpose of having me sleep with her husband. It was all making sense now. She hadn't shown up at the airport making sure Brody and I could spend time alone. She'd played the poor dismayed wife on the swing, crying on my lap, hoping for sympathy, and plotted to leave us together at the bar. She had set the whole thing up!

My thoughts turned to Brody. The poor man had shown love and admiration all these years and all he'd got in return was grief and a big old F-you. I was drunk, pissed off, and ready to take my anger out on someone. The only person I knew at the bar who deserved a verbal tongue lashing was Chloe's friend, the spy. Looking around the bar, thinking I had cop-like intuition, I wondered which one she was. I had some choice words for her.

As I scoured the bar, looking for suspects, I noticed Brody and Emma had moved over to the dance floor. He was pulling off some nice dance moves despite his drunken state. The phone buzzed in my pocket, but I didn't answer. I knew it was Chloe calling to either apologize or continue her quest, probably the latter. She would persist until she got her way.

I gave up the hunt; it was almost impossible to decipher which woman was reporting back to Chloe, although I had mentally noted a few possible culprits. I sat in silence, my mind still reeling from the fact that Chloe had had the audacity to ask me to sleep with Brody. I was lost in my thoughts when I felt a tap on my shoulder and looked up. It was Emma, looking cheerful.

"I finally beat him at pool, but I have to admit I had the advantage. I'm claiming it as a victory anyhow!" From the smile on her face, it was evident she admired Brody. "Although he eventually would've let me win anyhow. He gives people mercy wins; he's always thinking of others. I sure admire that man." She looked towards the dance floor smiling in Brody's direction. "He's so caring and kind. When we were growing up he always treated us well, my brother and me." She sighed, knitting her brow. "I didn't always have it easy; my dad was a drunk and would beat me and my brother often."

I was surprised she was talking so openly; she hardly knew me. The alcohol had obviously loosened her tongue and I was happy to hear more about Brody. She talked fast, continuing the story. "After my mom left, Dad often complained we were a burden and he didn't have enough money to support us. When he drank, it got worse, and we ended up suffering the brunt of his anger. He'd push us around or make us go to bed without supper. Once, he hit me after I tried to sneak into the kitchen to grab a piece of bread. I still recall the hunger pains sometimes." She gently rubbed her stomach at this point, the painful memory obviously still vivid in her mind.

"My dad insisted money was tight. We had to ration our portions, and he sent me to bed crying. The next day, he punished me further with no breakfast. I was starving and remember looking in the trash for something to eat. It was awful!" Her blue eyes paled from the recollection.

I shook my head in disbelief.

"I went to school extremely hungry and with a large bruise on my arm," Emma swallowed hard, a frown at the edge of her lips. "Nobody cared enough to ask until I ran into Brody after school." A smile returned at the memory. "After a few minutes of coaxing, reluctantly I told him about my abusive father. He wanted to know if my dad hit my brother too and I told him yes. My brother and Brody are best friends and I could tell he was concerned for him too. He told me he was going to take care of it. I never thought much of it, figuring he was just trying to make me feel better." She took a sip of her beer before carrying on.

"About a month later, Brody and his father showed up at my house. They discussed earnestly with my dad on the front steps for over an hour before handing him an envelope. My dad seemed emotional and hugged them. After that, the abuse stopped." She looked over at the dance floor again, her eyes fixed on Brody. "I found out last year, before my father passed away—the envelope was filled with money. I heard Brody's father had loaned him the money with the understanding he'd pay it back. I never understood why he missed so many school dances, sports, and activities… he was working on the farm, paying back the money. He did it to keep my brother and me safe; that's Brody. He's always helping people under the radar, in some way or another."

She sipped her beer and continued to look adoringly over in Brody's direction. "I can't believe I'm admitting this to a complete stranger but if he were single I'd chase him till the cows came home. No pun intended." She slapped her knee, poking fun at her joke. Emma was pretty, innocent and sweet. *Why hadn't Brody fallen in love with her?* "But seriously," she continued, her words earnest, conviction on her face, "I wouldn't relent until he was mine. Brody could have any woman in town, but he'd never think of cheating on Chloe." She waved her hand around the room for effect. "Many women have tried to break his resolve, but all have failed."

I sat in awe, so focused on Emma and her story I didn't see Brody walk over.

"What are you two lovely ladies talking about? Why the serious face, Bree?"

"Oh, just about how wonderful you are," Emma declared, piping in, giving him a quick, friendly kiss on the cheek.

"Thanks, kiddo. Not sure what brought on the compliment, but I'll take it." He tousled the top of her hair like a father would his child.

"Wanna play another round of pool?" She stretched her arms, pretending to prepare herself for another victory.

"I'll have to take a rain check and sit this one out. The room is starting to spin."

"You're just worried you're going to lose again, aren't you?" She playfully wrinkled her nose, pretending to be upset.

"Agreed," he conceded, bowing out gracefully.

Emma was satisfied with his admittance of defeat and skipped off to the pool table, looking for her next victim.

Once she was out of range, he questioned, "Why the long face? Looks like it's my turn to cheer you up?"

"Indeed, it is. Indeed, it is." I spontaneously leaned over and hugged him, enjoying the feeling of his warm chest against mine; it felt good. Chloe was going to get her wish after all.

Chapter 11
In for a Penny, In for a Pound

I WAS SURPRISED WITH MY SUDDEN CHANGE OF heart, but after Emma's story, I knew Brody deserved better, and Chloe would never leave him. She would keep stringing him along. I feared he'd be stuck in turmoil for years. As always, I was certain she wanted the perception of perfection and needed an excuse to leave him. By using me to tempt Brody, she'd have the perfect excuse— a cheating husband.

The only problem: he'd never sleep with me or anyone else for that matter. Emma had made it abundantly clear! What Chloe didn't realize and had failed to plan for was very evident: Brody had morals and ethics. He was not the kind of guy to lower himself to cheating, no matter how terrible things were at home. I needed to implement my own plan… it was going to involve more drinks.

"Another round please," I nodded at the bartender, showing him two fingers as I released Brody from my hug.

"Thanks for the hug but what was that about?" He was smiling, looking confused at the same time.

"Nothing much, just wanted to let you know I'll take care of things this time." He studied me, but did not ask for clarification, probably chalking it up to the liquor.

Brody had taken care of so many people under the radar; I was going to return the favor. The bartender placed two shooters on the bar, China Whites; he already knew what I liked. We each grabbed one, hooked arms, tilted our heads back, and let the creamy beverage slide down our throats.

"Delicious! Those are my favorite." I licked my lips. Noticing a small drop of liquor on his, I gently wiped it off with my finger. Curious, wanting confirmation, I experimented; placing my finger in my mouth I slowly sucked it clean. He watched but didn't take the bait. Instead, he continued with our conversation, not acknowledging my attempt at seduction. I respected him even more.

"I know! We've had a few of them already. Nice choice. Tonight's the first time I down a China White. I like the touch of cinnamon on top. That's pretty fancy stuff for around here. Maybe I need to play the part." He adjusted his collar and buttoned up his shirt. I laughed. "Although I fear the cream liqueurs are not mixing well with my beer and whiskey. Absolutely no more drinks for me. I'm cutting myself off." He groaned.

I nudged his ribs. "Try to keep up, farm boy."

"Are you making me out to be a wimp?"

"Perhaps I am." I tried to wink, a skill I never mastered, and it came off looking like I was having a seizure in my right eye. We bent over in laughter.

"Nice. You pick up many guys with that wink?"

"And I wonder why I'm single . . ." I put my hands in the air and shrugged.

"Why *are* you single?" His tone was more serious now.

"Broken heart. Still on the mend. I'm getting there. It's just taking longer than I'd hoped."

"Who broke your heart? I'll break his nose too." He winked, a much sexier wink than the one I'd accomplished.

"Your wink is sexier than mine," I remarked, changing the subject.

"You think my wink is sexy?" He looked surprised. "It's been a long time since anyone's mentioned any part of me as sexy." He smiled awkwardly but winked again. I enjoyed his innocent humor.

"You can't get a girl like Chloe without being sexy."

At the mention of his wife, his face dropped, the smile disappeared. Precisely what I wanted; I'd been looking for an opportunity to bring up her name. My plan required copious amounts of alcohol flowing through Brody's veins and I knew talking about Chloe would get him drinking again. I continued my barrage.

"Remember you mentioned earlier something about Chloe *not* being the cheating type?"

"Yes, I remember. Why do you bring it up?" He groaned and was looking fearful again; his budding cat-like characteristics no longer present.

"Just curious. What makes you think she wouldn't cheat?" I questioned, playing coy.

"I don't know. Men are very attracted to her and we sometimes fight about it, but I don't think she'd ever step out on me." He sounded more hopeful than convinced.

As he contemplated the thought of Chloe cheating, he hungrily took a beer I'd ordered for him.

I unmercifully posed hurtful questions: *Why did your wife leave the tavern with Caleb and not you? Where are they? What are they doing?* Over the next hour his fine motor skills dissipated with each beer.

By this time, I had sobered up, for the most part, and Brody was in the lead, five beers to my one. Distracted with thoughts of his wife he hadn't noticed my decline in consumption.

The live band announced it would be playing its last song and the bartender turned on a couple lights, warning the crowd it was almost closing time.

"Ok, enough Chloe-talk. Want to dance?" Brody nodded and started to stand, but stumbled backward into his chair.

"Woah, cowboy! Let me help you out." I grabbed his arm to steady his balance.

I had achieved my goal; he was intoxicated, barely able to stand, and at the level of impairment I needed to succeed. I supported him as we slowly walked over to the dance floor. I could feel the weight of his body leaning on me heavily throughout the song, and despite my smaller size, I was able to help him through the entire slow dance without incident. As the singer hummed the last words of the song, all the lights came on, illuminating the once-dark room. The beneficiaries of the free drinks guarded their eyes like vampires hiding from the sun.

"That's our cue. Time to head home."

"You're the boss," he slurred. "Do you think Chloe is home yet? I sure hope Caleb got his nose fixed."

This guy was too nice for his own good. I could see him asking about Chloe, but he worried about Caleb too ???

"I'm sure Chloe looked after him," I retorted sarcastically.

He groaned as we walked off the dance floor; his face sickly green. He looked like he was on the verge of vomiting. The mixture of beer, whiskey, and cream liquors was apparently coming back to haunt him. Bending over slightly, he steadied himself. He breathed in deeply and the greenish tinge faded.

I took his hand leading the way out. "Let's get you home."

"Agreed." Brody tried to straighten up, but instead went off balance and fell into a table cluttered with beer bottles. They tumbled over, a few landing on the tiles beneath, shattering all over the dance floor.

"Shit, did I make the mess?" he slurred.

"You've spent enough coin at this bar tonight. I'm sure they won't mind cleaning up your mess."

Brody had given the bartender nine hundred dollars. I helped with a four-hundred-dollar tip. I wasn't worried about a few broken beer bottles; it was the nature of the business.

I wrapped my arm around his slender waist and helped him off the table. I could feel his toned back against my arm. I admired the strength he had acquired from the long hours tending his farm. He was solid and very attractive on so many levels. What was Chloe possibly thinking, wanting to rid herself of this fine specimen of a man? He'd given her everything she wanted, but then again, she always liked what she couldn't have. Perhaps he no longer presented a challenge for her... Perhaps she was bored...

At any rate, it was time to get Brody home. I had started something I needed to finish it. As my mom would always say, "If you're in for a penny, you're in for a pound."

I was going for the pound—determined to get into Brody's pants.

Chapter 12
Thumbs up!

GRAVEL PINGED OFF THE CAB'S UNDERCARRIAGE ON the ride home. The sound made me nostalgic for my childhood in Nova Scotia. I had traveled many country roads in my dad's truck and loved the sound of the gravel hitting the underbelly of his truck. At that moment, I longed to be a kid again, free from the burdens of adulthood, free from the burden of what I was about to do.

Brody and I were in the backseat, his head leaning on my shoulder. He'd passed out shortly after I'd managed to load him into the cab. I laid my hand on his knee and felt an overwhelming need to protect him. We had become close and I considered him a friend. In the short time I'd known Brody, I felt like I knew him better than I did Chloe. With Brody, what you saw was what you got! He was uncomplicated compared to his wife. I knew opposites attracted and this was certainly the case with Brody and Chloe.

It had been about twenty minutes since we'd left the tavern and I could already see the lights of the farmhouse as we approached. They were beacons in the dark, guiding us home. With no street lights to brighten our way I was happy to be a passenger. I was a city girl, accustomed to bright lights and the luxury of electronic mapping devices. Our driver turned down Brody's long driveway and the change in direction woke him momentarily. He shifted his head off my shoulder and into my lap, trying to get comfortable; he looked peaceful. I couldn't resist running my fingers through his silky coiffed hair, as I had done to Chloe on the porch swing earlier that evening. I had been Chloe's comfort, and now I was his.

The cab pulled up to the front of the farmhouse. Chloe's Jeep was nowhere in sight. *Good*, I thought, *the second step was complete.* The first step had been getting him extremely drunk and the second step was making sure Chloe wasn't around. I was two for two. As I leaned forward to pay the cab driver, Brody's head tipped forward and he woke up.

"We're here," I informed.

He sat up, getting his bearings, then looked at his house with fondness. "Home sweet home," he said affectionately, smiling ear to ear.

I had grown partial to his sexy smile and took a moment to marvel at him, reluctant to start the final phase of my plan.

Brody fumbled with the cab's door handle, unable to open it. The cab driver jumped out quickly to assist. Brody, who'd been leaning on the door, tumbled out when it opened unexpectedly. *Maybe I've done too good of a job on step one?*

The cabbie, who I knew as Rex from his driver's identification card on the dashboard, helped Brody to his feet and up the front steps. When we reached the front door, Rex handed Brody over to me. I could have managed, but being from a small town, Rex had been anxious to help. I thanked him and gave him an extra thirty.

"Wow! Thanks!" Rex gushed, surprised by my generosity.

"I'm sorry for all the trouble and really appreciate your help."

"Well it's not too often I get to help Brody. Usually he's too busy helping others."

"Well it appears everyone in this town seems to have the same opinion of Brody."

"Yup, pretty much, he's very well liked." Rex leaned in and whispered into my ear, "Unlike his wife."

I nodded, knowing what he was referring to.

"Well, I'd better head back to the bar. We've only got two cabbies in town and I'm sure we have a few more people wanting to catch a ride home. Sometimes the locals get tired of waiting for a cab and end up driving. It's always a good idea to stay off these back roads late at night . . . if you know what I mean."

I nodded. "Drive safely, then."

"That's mighty kind of you. I hope you enjoy the rest of your time in Canada."

"I'm sure I will. All the best to your family."

During the ride back to the farmhouse, Rex had talked relentlessly about his immigration to Canada. He had already experienced the tragedy of losing his parents to war when he was only a boy. Luckily, he and his grandparents survived, and they'd moved to Canada shortly after. He was twenty now, and the wounds were slow to heal. He was hoping to become a police officer eventually, contributing to society by helping people and making a difference. I had been his captive audience for the entire ride, but I didn't mind. I waved good-bye as he got into the cab and Rex honked the horn in acknowledgment.

Brody was sandwiched between the door frame and my left hip. He'd already fallen asleep again. I had propped him into the position to keep him steady while I was saying good-bye to Rex. I opened the door. It was unlocked. No one in Bellevue locked their doors; it was a very safe and trusting community.

Brody was half-awake now, dragging his feet like stumps as I guided him to the living room couch. Upon arrival, he sat down, slumped over to his side, and fell back asleep. I arranged him into a comfortable position then stepped back, taking him all in. I sure hoped Chloe knew what she was doing. I was finally alone with Brody, which was the third and final stage of my plan. I had him exactly where I wanted him but I remained frozen, unable to move, unconvinced I was making the right decision.

When I was at the tavern, it had been easy to feel brave and heroic, alcohol enhancing my powers. But now, when faced with the reality of what I was about to do, I wasn't so brave. I felt more like a turtle wanting to seek refuge in its shell. Seeds of doubt entered my mind. *Did Brody really need my help? Who was I to interfere? Maybe they could work it out?*

I looked around the room, hoping to find any indication, a sign I was doing the right thing. Nothing. The only thing staring back at me was their wedding photo. They looked blissfully happy. Chloe was scooped up in Brody's arms, and they were both smiling at each other, like nothing else in the world mattered. I picked up the photo and ran my fingers over their faces, reconsidering. *They can work this out. Chloe really doesn't want this. How can she?* My phone buzzed. It was a message from Chloe. The message contained no words only an image, a thumbs up sign.

I was wrong.

She did want this.

Chapter 13
Wolf in Sheep's Clothing

BEFORE I COULD CONVINCE MYSELF OTHERWISE, knowing Brody would someday be thanking me for my actions, I did the unimaginable. I slowly removed my Gators t-shirt and let it drop to the floor. I made no sudden movements, taking care to be extremely quiet, not wanting to disturb him. He was passed out, but I was still nervous he might wake up.

The warm summer air was thick on my bare skin. I reached to the front of my black bra, unlatching the clasp between my breasts, delicately removing the garment, and then placing it on my top. My exposed nipples reacted to the breeze from the kitchen window, a refreshing and welcome break from the heat.

The whole situation felt wrong. I was mentally battling an ethical war but doing a better job this time keeping it at bay. I needed something to help initiate my plan. Something impure. Something to get myself in the mood. Then it came to me... Adam.

I started thinking about my ex-lover and our last time together. He had been a gentle lover and our lovemaking had gone on for hours. Oh, how I missed the touch of his hands on my body, the words of affection he'd whisper in my ear as we made love. I quickly became aroused, slowly moving my hands over my breasts and along my toned abdomen, letting my soft touch soothe and distract my thoughts. A tingling started between my legs as I imagined Adam inside me.

My thoughts were suddenly interrupted when Brody began to stir. I stood motionless and held my breath. He settled into a more comfortable position and breathed deeply once more. I let out a breath and my shoulders relaxed. *Would he be aroused if he woke to see me naked and touching myself? Probably not*, I concluded. He'd be more surprised than sexually inspired. Brody was a one-woman kind of man.

The moral dilemma of the situation crept its way into my head again. Before it took hold, I refocused. Thinking of Adam, I continued to trace my way downwards, slipping my hand into my jeans. I swiftly found the spot I was looking for and massaged it gently, my excitement evident from the moistness on my panties. Burning lust built up inside; I moaned. It was time. I was ready...

Removing my jeans and matching black panties, dropping them near my t-shirt and bra, I stood completely naked in front of Brody, only two feet between us. I looked up and caught my reflection in the living room window and marveled at myself. I knew I was desirable but Brody would resist. I slinked toward the couch, taking in a deep breath to calm myself, and then I slowly began to undo Brody's jeans. After a few slow and deliberate movements, I was able to methodically inch his jeans and boxers down to his knees.

Exhausted from my efforts, breaking into a light sweat, I knelt beside him, taking a few minutes to assess the totality of my actions, but my conclusion was the same: Chloe wanted this.

Mustering up the courage for my final assault, I thought, *this is for the best; their lives will be better for it.* I reached over and pulled my jeans closer to me, taking the phone from my front pocket and typing into the key pad, "Are you sure?"

My text was answered instantaneously. "Very."

"Then you know what to do."

I got up and stood over Brody, who was lying half-naked on the couch, the lower half of his body exposed. I hadn't noticed his manhood when removing his boxers; I'd been too distracted with the ethical dilemma of my task. I took a few moments to admire his girth. I procrastinated, not wanting to bridge the gap.

I felt like a wolf in sheep's clothing, although I had none on, coming into his house and taking advantage of him, helping his wife end their marriage. Enough! It was time!

I slowly and carefully mounted Brody and started to rock myself against his manhood. It took over a minute before his body responded. I ran my fingers through his thick brown hair and along his toned chest, grinding myself into him harder. I could feel him growing against my thigh. He started to moan Chloe's name, his eyes still firmly shut, enjoying the sensation. He reached up and cupped my breasts. His eyes flashed open when he realized they didn't belong to his wife.

A look of horror and shock spread across his face. "What are you doing, Bree?" He started to push me off, but it was too late.

At that moment, Chloe walked through the door—on cue—and started to sob.

Chapter 14
Come as a Friend—Leave as a stranger

CHLOE PLAYED HER ROLE AS THE DISTRAUGHT WIFE impeccably well and I was headed for the next flight home. My job was done. I called for a cab and luckily enough Rex answered the phone. I was overwhelmed by the situation and asked him to come pick me up as soon as possible.

Brody was bewildered and confused, pleading with me to tell Chloe what I had done, but I refused to say a word for fear I would cave and spill the truth. I had an urge to do so but knew I had to stay strong for his sake. Thankfully, Rex arrived in record time and I rushed out of the house. There were no good-byes. No bear hugs. Just the sound of Chloe crying and Brody imploring his defence. When their front door shut behind me, I felt relief. I had become the unwanted guest, a stark contrast from my arrival—a friend turned stranger.

It had only been about an hour and a half since Rex dropped us off. He hopped out of the cab, ran to the passenger door, and opened it for me. "After you, my lady," he insisted, as I handed him my suitcase then jumped into the cab. He closed the door quickly behind me, sensing I was in a rush, and loaded my suitcase in the trunk. I wanted to get as far away from Chloe as I could. I was anxious to put distance between us and to get back to the comfort of my condo, leaving the whole mess behind.

Rex hopped into the driver's seat and as we started to pull away, I dared to look back—I could see Chloe through the large living room window, crying on the couch, head in her hands, Brody frantically waving his hands in the air, pleading with her.

I could still hear his many protests: "I didn't touch her! I don't know what happened! She was trying to have sex with me! I didn't do a thing!"

And then Chloe screaming accusingly at him, "You're a disgusting cheat and liar . . . like she just *fell* on your dick!" She was an excellent actress, crumpling herself into a ball on the couch, crying uncontrollably, and just as quickly screaming at him in rage . . . an Oscar-winning performance.

I turned my thoughts and attention away from them and onto Rex to change the disastrous scenery inside my head. I felt only time would tell if I'd made the right decision. Rex was looking at me through his rear-view mirror. He could see I was visibly upset.

"Leaving so soon? Weren't you supposed to be staying another few days?"

"Yeah, something came up suddenly. I have to get back home."

"Hmmm . . . everything OK?" His voice expressing the concern I'd had for him, worried he was sharing the road with drunk drivers.

"It will be soon," I said with resolve.

Rex didn't ask any more questions and changed the subject, talking about law enforcement classes instead. I was half-listening this time. My thoughts were pulled back to Brody and the ordeal I had set in motion for him. I kept telling myself it was for the best, but after seeing him in chaos, I was doubting myself. I knew it was going to take some time before he got his life back on track, but I hoped he'd be happier for it. I also hoped he'd never find out the truth about the setup because it would hurt him even more. I never wanted him to know his wife had solicited her best friend to sleep with him.

While I was at the tavern getting Brody drunk, I'd managed to break away, claiming I needed to use the bathroom. Instead, I'd called Chloe in a moment of bravery.

"I'll do it!" I whispered, not wanting any of the visitors within the confines of the bathroom to overhear.

"What changed your mind?" She asked stunned, obviously surprised by my sudden change of heart.

"The thought of him being stuck with you the rest of his life!" I seethed into the phone.

Normally, she would have taken offence to such a comment, but she needed my help. "So now what?"

"Get home now! I've got it all under control. Just stay hidden out of sight on the back porch. I'll text you when we're in the cab"

She had been extremely happy to hear my plan and during the cab ride home, while Brody slept on my shoulder and Rex chatted about his time in Canada, we planned his undoing over several text messages.

"We're in the cab," I texted Chloe.

A few seconds later, my screen lit up with her response. "How will I know when?"

"I'll text you. Walk through the front doors EXACTLY three minutes later, NOT a second more!"

I was convinced Brody would never cheat on her, luckily, because I had no intentions of sleeping with him. I knew once I had him in a compromising position, it wouldn't last long. We needed to time her entrance to a *tee*.

"I owe you one." Chloe even had the nerve to add a smiley face.

I didn't have anything to add. She had tested my patience and I had other priorities; getting into Brody's pants. Our plan had worked perfectly, and now she was on her way to becoming a free woman and I was on my way home.

Rex was still chatting, and his happy demeanor brought me back to the present. "You folks sure have been keeping me busy tonight. This is the third time I've been to Brody's farmhouse tonight. First, I brought Chloe home, about half an hour before you arrived. Then you and Brody, and now you again. I might have to start giving discounts," he joked. "Why didn't you three save some money and travel back together?"

I knew the answer to his question but couldn't tell him. Chloe had returned in a separate cab to hide until I got her husband in a sexually vulnerable position. I couldn't tell him I felt like a liar and cheat, yet somehow a hero too. It made no sense to me, let alone to a stranger. I was certain he'd heard his share of stories while chauffeuring around drunken customers, but this one would probably top them all. I had no intentions of outing Chloe, but knew I'd need time to heal from the inflictions she'd caused, shaming me to end her marriage.

Instead, I answered, "Oh, she was tired and wanted to head back home, so she left before us."

"Well, I'm sure you'll be back soon," he ventured.

"Probably not for a while." I changed the subject to his family, which he gladly talked about until we arrived at the airport. Rex dropped me off at the same gate Brody had picked me up from not twenty-four hours earlier.

I walked through the revolving door, shaking my head in dismay, thinking, *I never thought my trip to Canada would involve my longest and truest friend asking me to be her husband's 'mistress' and most of all me accepting!* The automatic door spat me out. I wheeled my luggage to the nearest sales wicket and purchased the first ticket to New York.

As I was walking through the airport, I received a call from Chloe. "It worked. I told him I was leaving him, and he's already agreed. He's blaming himself for the whole thing. I don't know how I can ever repay you. I owe you *big* time!"

I gripped my phone tightly and spat out my words; frustrated and upset. "What we did was cruel and shameless, but he'll be better off without you. As for my repayment," I commanded, "you're only taking one third of his money. Plus, you're telling everyone it was a mutual decision to leave each other. You will *not* claim he cheated on you. You got what you wanted, a divorce! No one must be the 'bad guy'! If I hear you're deviating from this part of the deal, I will tell Brody the truth and show him the text messages to prove it."

"Well, haven't you become my husband's, or should I say *ex*-husband's, guardian angel? I like the sound of that: *ex*-husband." She guffawed, clearly not taking offence to any of my comments. She didn't care; she seemed extremely happy to have her way. She was in charge now; I suspected Brody would do her bidding because he felt so guilty. I hung up on her for the second time that evening, feeling worn out and tired. I rubbed my eyes, fighting off sleep. It was almost five in the morning and my body ached for rest.

I held back the tears. I reached into my bag to put away my phone and felt a soft material. *What?* I pulled it out. *Oh, yeah*. It was the Gators t-shirt I'd wanted to give her as a birthday gift. A few tears escaped as I threw it in the trash and headed for the departure gate.

Chapter 15
The Aftermath

OVER THE NEXT TWO MONTHS, I MADE SURE CHLOE held up her end of the bargain. She assured me Brody was not black-listed as the bad guy. Instead, she told the community of Bellevue a different, less scandalous story: they'd agreed to separate for mutual reasons.

Conscious of what Chloe was capable of, it stood to reason my trust in her wavered. I relied on some of my old friends in Bellevue to confirm her story; she remained true to her word.

Chloe had also made some changes, replacing Caleb with the local vet, Trevor, whom she'd had on speed dial. She complained about not getting as much money as she had hoped after the separation and picked the rich guy over Caleb the cupcake. She figured Trevor was probably a better match anyhow because he didn't want kids; he preferred animals. Besides, she was sure they were in love—already talking about marriage.

Shortly after ensuring Brody's reputation was intact, I stopped taking Chloe's calls. I was hurting; her betrayal added to the sting of Adam's infliction.

As for Brody, I heard his best friend's kid sister, Emma, was working periodically with him on the farm. They were not dating, Brody was still healing, but perhaps they were setting the groundwork for something in the future. Apparently, she wanted lots of kids—maybe Brody would finally get the family he deserved.

I took comfort in knowing things were starting to work out for Brody. I wasn't proud of myself for deceiving him, but I was satisfied to have helped re-set his life, having acted as a sort of unusual guardian angel. And oddly enough, the experience had helped me too. For once, I'd managed to set things right. I'd been the "good" mistress, so to speak! Without realizing it, I was slowly healing, forgiving myself. Unbeknownst to me, I'd already started down a new path in life, one I'd never imagined.

Chapter 16
Samantha

I'D JUST STEPPED OFF THE TREADMILL AFTER A FIVE kilometer run. My t-shirt was moist and sweat dripped from my brow. My cell phone rang. I wiped my hands on the standard white towels provided by the gym, ridding my hands of any moisture before answering the phone. It was a few months after the Canada trip and I had been using the gym more regularly; it helped release any residual frustrations toward Chloe. A private caller. I didn't answer, thinking it was a telemarketer. It seemed they were the only people who called using private or blocked numbers. On the fifth ring, the caller gave up.

I walked over to the free weight station and started the second half of my workout when it rang again. Private number. I answered, annoyed; my workout was being disturbed, yet again.

"Yes." I expected a salesperson on the other end, trying to sell some useless item I didn't need.

"Hello, my name is Samantha. I got your number from Chloe. Is this Bree?"

Her voice was soft, I could barely hear what she was saying. The loud music, plaguing the gym, also interfered with our conversation. I was becoming increasingly annoyed, but she had my attention. Why was a stranger calling and why had Chloe given her my number? I was no longer in contact with Chloe. I had seen a side of her which repulsed me. I had lots of friends and didn't need one like her.

"Yes," I confirmed, as I walked over to a quieter spot, near the gym's entrance way.

"Can you talk?" she whispered, speaking even more quietly.

"About what exactly?" I wished she'd get to the point.

Reading my thoughts, she said, "I'll get straight to the point… Chloe told me about what you *did* for her and I was wondering if you could do the same for me. I'll pay generously for your help."

I couldn't believe it. Chloe had done it again, thrown me under the bus! And what was this woman doing, wanting to compensate me for trying to sleep with her husband? I didn't know if I should be insulted or laugh. I was silent, taking in everything she was saying.

"He cheats on me and I can't catch him. He's much too careful and clever. Chloe sent me your picture. He won't be able to resist you. My husband isn't a good man like Brody."

She obviously knew Brody well. My thoughts went to him. I had recently heard things had improved for Brody; he was dating. A thought passed through my mind. *Maybe I can help her too!*

"How much?" I queried out of curiosity, thinking she'd come in at a couple thousand.

"Twenty-five thousand dollars. Would it be fair?"

My mouth dropped open. Twenty-five thousand dollars! That was a lot of money. It sure would be nice! No longer had the thought entered my mind when it flipped from money to the ethical aspect of her request. I had done it for Chloe but that had been different. There had been no deliberate planning until a few hours before, well at least not on my part. I now knew Chloe had invited me to go to Canada for the sole purpose of setting up her husband.

I wasn't sure what to say. My brain was still trying to process her request. Samantha sensed my hesitation. "I need your help, Bree. Please. I don't have anyone else I can trust with this. I need you to be my husband's... mistress."

"His *mistress*? I'm *not* going to sleep with him!" I hadn't reconciled the thought of myself as an 'official mistress' for hire at this point.

"I know, Chloe mentioned that part. I just need proof he'd cheat on me and it doesn't necessarily involve you sleeping with him. I just want to know if he's willing to have an affair and I need a mistress for hire to prove it. I've spent thousands on private investigators, but they were never able to get close enough. I have several photos of him with three different women but never in *compromising positions*. I need one hundred percent proof before I leave him."

Was she local? "Where do you live?" I asked, curiosity getting the best of me.

"Nevada."

"I always wanted to see Nevada," I admitted jokingly.

"Then please come. I need you. I need closure."

Samantha pleaded her case for the next few minutes before I told her I had to think it over and would call her the next day with an answer. She gave me her number, we hung up and I headed back to the treadmill, needing some adrenaline to help process the information and perhaps shed some light on the situation.

Each time my foot hit the treadmill, my thoughts became clearer, like a set of dominoes falling in order, one after another. I wanted to stop women like me—men like Adam. I owed it to karma and to myself.

I felt it would finally help me heal. I desperately wanted to love the woman I used to be. And becoming a mistress for hire would help me do just that!

Only one question remained as I stepped off the tread-mill: was I willing to get down and dirty again, sexually compromising myself to help this woman? I grappled with it until my head hit the pillow that night.

In bed, staring at my cream-colored walls, I examined the decorative floral painting I'd received from my mother as a house-warming gift. I wasn't very fond of the dark purple, but knew better than to remove it. I'd be facing her wrath. My mother's inquiries about its absence wouldn't stop until it found its place back on the wall. My eyes followed the flow of the stems as I made mental notes of what I would be willing to do sexually if I did take the job. After careful consideration I'd come up with a list—it was short—flirt, kiss, fondle, get naked.

I was willing to put myself in an uncomfortable sexual situation, as I had done for Chloe, but just long enough to confirm her beliefs. It was necessary to get the evidence she needed to prove what she suspected. I was willing to do this to help her find answers. He was already cheating on her; she just couldn't catch him. Here was a woman needing my help to end a relationship she felt she could not leave until she could confirm his infidelity.

My decision was just about made in her favor, but I needed a little something extra to push me into a definite yes . . . then it came to me. I took my phone from the bedside table and looked up Brody on social media. *Is he truly happy?* From what others had told me, he was, but I needed to see for myself. As I scrolled through his photos, I came across one he had posted the day before. Brody was sitting on the hood of his truck with Emma by his side, smiling ear to ear, and the caption read, "Life is good."

It was official. My decision was made.

Chapter 17
A Mistress, hired

I WOKE THE NEXT MORNING FEELING RESTED AND content and for the very first time found myself admiring my mother's floral painting! It was amazing how my perception on life had improved overnight. I was happier than I had been in a long time; my new job was giving me a renewed sense of purpose. I felt like my life was finally heading in the right direction. After a year of trying to mend my broken heart and forget about Adam, I had something to really take my mind off the pain, something to help me heal.

I strolled over to the kitchen in my plush rose-colored bathrobe, feeling relaxed, not wanting to rush any of my sentiments away. Although I wasn't much of a cook, I enjoyed spending time in the kitchen. It wasn't anything fancy but it suited my needs. The off-white cupboards complimented the small space, making it look larger than it was. The pantry was filled with all sorts of kitchen appliances, which I never used and had bought on an impulse, hoping one day I'd take up cooking like my grandmother. She was an excellent cook and didn't use cookbooks or watch any fancy cooking shows like I did. Her recipes were made from a pinch of this and a dab of that.

When my grandparents had come to visit my condo for the first time, a few years earlier, I was in admiration as I watched them walk around my tiny abode hand in hand, nodding in approval. The only thing in my home to receive a disapproving eye from grandma—my kitchen gadgets, but I didn't mind. I knew she meant well and I didn't expect an expert chef such as herself to understand. They stayed for tea and left the same way they had come, holding hands. I ached for a relationship like theirs.

I reached for my favorite mug, a giant aqua coffee cup the size of a bowl, taking it by the dolphin-shaped handle. It was a trinket I'd picked up at a thrift shop. Its fanciful colors reminded me of the ocean and I'd been drawn to it immediately. Two quarters, and then it was mine. Filling it with coffee and two table spoons of vanilla cream, I sipped slowly. When I'd finished my morning breakfast—yes, that was my breakfast!—I decided it was time to call Samantha.

My stomach flipped and flopped as I waited for her to answer the phone. Although I was feeling confident with my decision, it was still a little unsettling to "officially" become someone's mistress for hire, but I was slowly coming to terms with my new title.

"Hello?" she murmured, her words soft and faint.

"Hi, Samantha. It's Bree."

"Oh, Bree, I'm so happy to hear from you." Her tone picked up a beat. "Thanks for calling back. I was worried I'd scared you away. You've made my day."

"I'm glad to hear it!"

"And . . ." she probed, ever so politely.

"Yes. I'll do it."

"Yes. You'll do it!" Samantha echoed my words, confirming them. "I can't express how much this means to me . . . to my family."

"I'll do whatever I can to help."

"It's settled then, and for your troubles I'm compensating you $30,000."

I protested. "We agreed on $25,000."

"I'm so excited to have you on board with *this* I've added an additional $5,000 to pay for your travel expenses to Nevada. It shouldn't come out of your fee," she said firmly.

I agreed, with little hesitation. "I appreciate your generosity." Money was obviously not an issue for her.

"So, when can you come? Two days from now? Or is it too soon?"

The timing was perfect, the Chic Chick was being shut down for two weeks because the bartenders—my dear Josh included—were serving alcohol to minors. The job offer came at the right time—I was short on cash.

"That would be great. It'd give me time to get things in order before leaving."

I hesitated, choosing my words wisely to make my next comment abundantly clear. "I need you to understand I'm not going to actually *sleep* with your husband. I'm willing to get physical with him, to some degree," my throat closed up, "but I am *not* a prostitute."

"You're more like an *aggressive* detective. This time around I needed to hire someone who could get me results. Like I mentioned before, I need pictures of him in compromising positions, nothing more and the sooner you get here the better."

Samantha suggested a few airlines, and we courteously said our good-byes.

I booked my flight to Nevada, set to arrive two days later. I called Samantha to give her the particulars—flight times and hotel. She thanked me, then expressed a concern with discussing things over the phone as her children were returning home. We decided to mull over the details upon my arrival.

I called my boss, telling him I would be out of town and returning to work by the time the club re-opened. Easy-going and laidback, he sent his well wishes, requesting only a bottle of rum to keep my spot.

I didn't know it then, but my life was changing. Things were happening . . .

My new career had officially started. I never worked at the Chic Chick again. And my new job was leading me closer and closer to . . . my soul mate.

Chapter 18
Willowdale, Nevada

WHEN I ARRIVED IN WILLOWDALE, NEVADA, TWO days later in the late evening, I felt at ease and ready to work, even though I still had an urge to hurry things along. Time was of the essence, with only two weeks to complete my task before needing to return to work at the club. Waving down a cab, I hopped in. "Hotel 7, please."

The young cabbie raced along the congested Nevada highway like a bat out of hell. Gripping the edge of the car door, bracing myself for another sharp turn, I hoped I wouldn't die! I could see the headlines now: "MISTRESS FOR HIRE, DEAD!"

Leafing through Samantha's emails on my phone, I found an e-transfer for $20,000, the remaining $10,000 to be provided when the evidence was in hand. I clicked on a second email which included a photo of herself alongside her husband, Evan, on their wedding day. Truth be told, he was a homely looking man . . . short, fat, and balding. Samantha looked much younger and more attractive, but that aside, they seemed to be in love—eyes locked, gazing at each other lovingly. But somewhere down the line, Evan's feelings must have changed, and the sentiment had since evaporated; hence my trip to Nevada.

The setting sun glowed orange behind the landscape, a beautiful backdrop to the shady motel just outside the city. I wasn't happy with Samantha's choice. She'd apologized for asking me to stay in such a dubious place, but she needed to make certain no one saw us together.

The motel—dilapidated, with peeling paint, drooping shingles, rusty signs, and a severely uneven driveway, had seen better days. One of the taxi's tires hit a large pothole on the way in, bouncing alarmingly. *It's only temporary*, I thought.

I checked in at the front desk with the older lady, her demeanor matching her surroundings: a shot of tough bourbon. I confirmed my two-week stay—I'd booked the maximum number of nights just in case it took a little longer than expected—then headed to my room.

As I set my suitcase on the bed, likely the cleanest spot in the room, there was a sudden knock at the door. I jumped, startled. I wasn't expecting company. I peered through the peep hole, curious, to find a figure in black standing in front of my doorway.

"Who is it?"

Pulling back her hood, Samantha revealed herself.

We had agreed to meet at the motel to go through her husband's schedule, to decide on the best place to make my approach, but that wasn't to be till later this evening. As I opened the door, she scooted into the room. In an effort to disguise herself, she wore black baggy pants, a dark hoodie, and a baseball cap pulled down low.

"Close the door quickly," she snapped, appearing stressed, nervous, and upset with the whole situation.

I closed the door in haste. I was surprisingly very calm. "You're early," I stated, smiling. "How did you find me? I was supposed to message you my room number once I had the chance to settle in."

"I was waiting in my car and followed you up to your room. I couldn't wait. I'm nervous and anxious about all this." She waved her hand around the room and at me, as if indicating the location and I were the source of her problems.

"I didn't even notice. You'd make a great detective." I made a mental note to be more aware of my surroundings in the future.

Samantha warmed to my compliment, seeming to relax. "It helps when you're beautiful. No one could miss the likes of you."

Whatever tension lurked in the room dissipated. I motioned for her to sit, and she chose the edge of the bed. *Good choice,* I thought. *You'll stay cleaner that way!* She had probably come to the same conclusion as I had about the bed.

I sat across from her, on the dingy-looking sofa chair with its tattered and worn cushions and mystery stains.

With the tension out of the way, we got down to business. I questioned her about her husband and their relationship. My questions sounded concise and professional. I surprised myself. *I'm a natural!* It helped I had rehearsed the questions during my flight and had been ready for her despite her early arrival. My goal was to get inside her husband's head. I needed to understand what made him tick.

She started with some basics, including his likes and dislikes. They had married four years ago, and were generally happy, or so she'd thought. The only issue that stood out in her mind was the prenuptial agreement she'd been forced to sign. At the time, she'd refused, explaining she could be trusted, but he called off the wedding until she conceded a few weeks later.

She shook her head and started playing with her fingernails, slowly ripping them off one by one and depositing them in her lap as she told her story. "He bought me diamonds, exotic trips, and expensive clothes after refusing to marry me unless I signed the papers, but no matter what he did, things had changed between us. It was never the same. The prenup caused an imaginary wall between us."

Looking forlorn and sad sitting on the edge of the motel room bed dressed all in black, she was a shadow of herself. I shook my head, perplexed by his actions, and encouraged her to go on.

"As you can tell, he's not very attractive, but it never mattered to me. He's awkward and socially inept and never had a committed relationship until he met me. You'd think with all his money he'd have been popular with the ladies, but he was too cheap, and they usually dumped him after the first date." Another nail landed on her lap, "When we started dating, he took me to inexpensive restaurants, the kind where he could redeem his coupons. He rarely parted with his money, but I continued to date him despite his thriftiness. I had a fantastic job and liked to pay my own way anyhow. I even paid for many of the dates myself. Evan eventually grew to trust me and realized I was not dating him for the money. Naturally, I was baffled when he told me about the prenuptial."

She sighed, and I remained silent, allowing her to continue when she was ready. After a few brief moments, she went on. "I married him regardless of his faults. I loved him for his humor and wit. I foolishly assumed he loved me too. I was wrong...six months ago, I found out about the *hookers* . . ." She breathed out slowly, the word "hookers" rolling off her tongue like a curse. "I was devastated. My world shattered."

"Hookers? You told me he cheated on you . . . but with hookers?" I said unable to hide the shock in my voice.

"I couldn't believe it either. I found out by mistake! Our accountant had called, asking me to forward some receipts he needed to complete our tax returns. I was in Evan's office, looking for them, when I came across his medical folder— stuffed with papers. I knew he'd only been to the doctor twice, so I was surprised to see so many receipts. Normally I would have left it, but I was naturally concerned and did a little digging. To make a long story short, he was receiving services from hookers, getting a receipt, and claiming it as a tax write off. Three different women issued them, all co-owners of a small therapeutic massage business in town. The same three women are in the photos taken by my private investigators. In one year my husband had over $33,000 in medical bills for 'therapeutic massages.' He's so cheap, he writes off his hookers! It's laughable," she scoffed.

"Unbelievable," I gasped. "He has no soul. You poor thing." I put my hand on her knee and she brushed it away.

"I don't need anyone feeling sorry for me," she leered, taking her frustrations out on the wrong person.

"I didn't mean to offend you."

"You didn't. I just don't want you taking pity on me." Crossing her arms over her chest, she subconsciously put a wall between us. She was upset, and I didn't blame her.

"OK, you're the boss!" I gave her a light punch on the arm, chancing it would make her laugh.

Luckily, she caught my drift and smirked. Tilting her head as she assessed me, she stated, "He's going to fall for you in no time flat. Not only are you beautiful but you're kind and sweet. I wish it didn't have to come to this, asking you for help, but I know he'll make my life a living hell if I leave him. I need undeniable proof for my sake and his mother's. I know he's very careful and sticks to the same three women: Bambi, Tiffany, and Bianca. Those were the names on the receipts anyhow. He pays them a decent price to keep their mouths shut. I've hired three investigators, but none were successful; they can't get close enough."

Not realizing Evan's mother was part of the equation, I wanted to know more. "Pardon my curiosity but you mentioned needing to prove it to his mother. Why is that?"

Already on fingernail number seven, Samantha went on to explain—her narcissistic mother-in-law worked tirelessly to keep up her perfect appearance within the community. Samantha knew her husband's wealth was sustained by his mother's generous deposits into his bank account. Evan's mother's rich lifestyle was acquired from her husband, who had owned a car dealership. When he'd died of a sudden heart attack several years back, Evan's mother was left with a huge fortune after selling the high-end dealership to an Asian company.

Before they were married, Evan lived in the guest house on his mother's property. Feeling sorry for her only child after his father passed away, she'd provided him with room and board, free of charge. He was a bachelor and lived like one, too—drinking lots, hosting parties. That's how they had met, at one of his parties.

Samantha had heard through the rumor mill, that Evan was living the life until his mother's friends, who were often at her house for tea, first began murmuring, then not-so-subtle questions, then very pointed questions about Evan's lifestyle to the point his mother could no longer ignore them. Too many questions about her son's partying and lack of spouse didn't reflect well on her. Embarrassed, she threatened to cut him off if he continued his wild bachelor ways. She wanted her forty-three-year-old baby to settle down.

He was to marry within the year, to a woman not more than eight years his junior, an age difference his mother believed to be socially acceptable. Anything more, and the deal was off—no money.

Shortly after Samantha heard the rumor they started dating. She was exactly eight years and eleven months his junior. They fell in love and were married. In the beginning, Samantha was convinced he loved her. Even then, she'd suppressed the niggling worry he had married her only to pacify his mother.

Their marriage wasn't quite what Samantha had imagined, being heavily influenced by his mother. While Evan hadn't wanted children when they first married, he'd changed his mind after his mother 'suggested' otherwise. All his mother's friends were becoming grandparents, and she was feeling left out. He—and Samantha—obliged, producing twin girls and a boy. While his mother was elated, she rarely visited the children. She had got what she wanted: grandchildren to brag about over tea.

After the children were born, Evan slowly returned to his previous partying ways, Samantha eventually realized he clearly hadn't been ready to settle down.

Even though there was a prenuptial in place, she knew Evan would be reluctant to let her leave. His mother had threatened to withdraw his cash flow if he ever tarnished her reputation—having a divorced son would do just that!

By this point, Samantha had pulled off the last of her nails. Collecting them into her hand, she got up, depositing the uneven pieces into the waste basket. She paced the room, increasingly anxious—silent for the longest time—suddenly she blurted out, "I know why he likes hookers."

"You do?" I tried not to sound surprised this time.

"If I tell you the story, you have to promise to never tell a soul." Her eyes darted around the room, like a rabbit ready to flee, danger everywhere.

I wasn't sure who she thought I would tell, but didn't ask. "You have my word."

"Seriously. No one can know. *No one!*"

"It's OK. I won't tell anyone. Promise." I instinctively put my hand on my heart, trying to reassure her I could be trusted.

She sighed, unable to meet my eyes, and picked at what remained of her jagged fingernail tips. "It started when . . ."

Chapter 19
Bad Evan!

WHEN SAMANTHA WAS PREGNANT WITH THE TWINS, she began to suspect Evan missed his old life as a wild bachelor. One night, after Evan had taken a strong prescription medication for a wrist injury he'd incurred the day before, he rambled on about his past. Normally a private man, rarely sharing anything with her, he didn't hold back that night.

* * *

Eight months pregnant and not in the mood, she lay beside him in bed, her pregnant belly against his back.

"I remember our first time together, meeting at one of my wild parties. I miss all the sex we used to have during those days." He turned to face her with a mischievous smile, cheerful at the thought. He placed a hand on her breast, testing the waters.

"I know this is going to take some getting used to, but we're going to be parents soon. Those days are over."

Samantha gingerly moved his hand away, her breasts tender from the hormones flowing through her body. She smiled playfully at him, hoping to let him down easy.

Evan's cheeks flushed a deep shade of crimson, revealing his anger at the rejection. He turned his back on her, curling into a ball away from her tentative touch. Her attempt to appease him rebuffed, Samantha closed her eyes, upset he didn't understand her needs.

Lying on the edge of the bed, one hand resting on her distended belly, Samantha considered the state of their marriage. She replayed moments of their romance, which had blossomed quickly, but he was right, shortly after he'd proposed, the parties—and their wild sex—had come to a stop. At first, he seemed fine with it, maybe because it was something new, but several months into their marriage, he started whining his life just wasn't the same. Samantha felt being his shiny new quarter, perfect to show all his mother's friends, had faded.

They seemed to be slowly drifting apart. They fought often, which frequently left her alone, both emotionally and physically. Finding excuses to leave their home after they fought, Evan would be gone for hours. The only reason he hadn't taken off in his truck that night was due to his being heavily medicated and he couldn't drive.

She placed a hesitant hand on the small of his back.

He jolted, then rolled to face her, a scowl on his face. "What?"

"Let's make love, like the old days."

His expression softened, and his anger seemed to dissipate. "I was hoping you'd change your mind. Turn over. Your belly has gotten too big! I need access from the back." He chuckled, liking his crude joke. Doing as he ordered, she placed herself in position. He pushed her panties to the side and entered her. Thrusting several times before finishing, then rolling on his back, he gloated, having got his way.

Readjusting her panties in place, content the ordeal was over, Samantha sighed, hoping he'd be satisfied for at least another week. His need to 'party' satisfied. She was wrong.

"I think we should host a party next week? What do you think?"

She couldn't believe his lack of empathy for her current state; she was set to have the babes in four weeks and he wanted a party! Carefully, treading water, not wanting to make any waves, she asked, "Baby, I'm curious, why your love for parties?"

Having bridged the gap with sex, and with the help of the pain meds, Evan was languid and talkative, and began theorizing about his love to party. Apparently, his father had enjoyed parties and women. This was the first time Samantha had ever heard Evan say anything negative about his father. He adored his father and would never tarnish his reputation, but that night, under the influence of pain killers, he blamed his father for his wild ways. Evan was convinced his deviancy started the summer he'd turned seventeen. He'd even written about it in a journal he kept hidden in his mom's guest house under the bar sink. Evan rambled on about his old abode, a place he cherished and missed, then fell asleep a few minutes later.

He lay snoring beside her, the sound unbearable keeping her awake. Placing her hands over her ears, desperate for sleep, she found herself thinking about his journal. *Why was it hidden? What had his father done? And why had it influenced Evan so much?* The air being forced from her husband's mouth sounded like a low-pitch creaky hinge on a door swaying in the wind. At that, she climbed out of bed and did what any reasonable curious wife would do. She drove to the guest house and found what she was looking for, precisely where he said it would be, under the bar sink. Drawing in a long breath, apprehensive of what she may find, she opened the journal and began to read.

* * *

He had come home from school over the lunch hour to pick up some pot he kept hidden under his bed in a piggy bank. His grandma had given him the piggy as a toddler— but it still had a purpose—hiding his 'goods.' Evan had known the house would be empty. Twice a week, during his lunch hour, he would raid the little pig of its' jewels. When he arrived home that day, he did what he had done so many times before: run up the front steps, punch in the code, and wait for the front door to click open.

Although he knew his parents weren't home, he always worried they might find his stash. His mother had threatened to take away his allowance if she ever caught him smoking weed. She'd found out from a friend at the country club that Evan's friends liked to smoke pot. His mother cared more about gossip than his bad habits—but none the less he was careful.

He was slim in those days and jetted up the massive wooden staircase which filled most of the foyer. He passed his parents' master bedroom, the gym, the entertainment room, and a large bathroom before finally arriving at his own bedroom. A large Metallica poster, tattered and torn, hung on the inside of his bedroom door. The corner of the tape had lost its sticking power and the poster was lopsided; he never bothered to fix things or clean up after himself; he left it for the maid.

The maid kept the house spotless and would do whatever he demanded. He threatened to have her fired when she refused to cut his toenails the week before. She ended up cutting them but wasn't happy about it. He had chuckled while telling the story to his friends, enjoying the thought of the maid having to concede to his request.

His large bedroom had already been cleaned up. His dirty laundry no longer littered the floor and his bed was made. He liked a messy room, but his mom would never allow it. The house needed to be tidy.

He strolled over to his car-shaped bed in the center of the room. He was much too old for it, but his mother refused to give it up. She held onto the notion giving up the bed would mean her little boy was all grown up—she wasn't ready.

Her brother, his uncle, had bought it for him on his third birthday. The king-sized bed was made of solid oak and designed to look like a Formula One race car. The price tag on the red bed had been hefty. It was custom-made at a high-end bedroom store in Paris, France, which provided furniture for spoiled rich kids.

When he had turned ten years old, the novelty of the bed had worn off and he'd wanted a replacement. His father had agreed, but his mother had not. His father never argued with his wife, so the bed remained.

Evan had let the issue drop until his friends started to ridicule him for having a child's bed. He protested again but his mother wouldn't relent, so he refused to sleep in the bed. Two weeks later, his mother compromised by having it painted black and doubled his allowance for his troubles. Evan knew by then she would never change her mind, so he took the money—relieved to no longer be sleeping on the floor.

Three times the size of a normal bedroom, his room was filled with old stuffed toys, video games, books, and other items littering the shelves of his bedroom. He was only interested in one thing—his piggy bank.

He reached under his bed in search of his treasure, but instead felt the smooth edges of dishware. He'd forgotten he'd shoved plates under his bed from his late-night snack the day before. He looked under the bed—mac and cheese dried onto a plate and a half-eaten bowl of chips lying on its side. He pulled the soiled dishes into the open, so the maid would see them. She knew better than to clean beneath the bed. He'd warned her it was off limits—hence the dirty dishes.

Searching, shrouded by the car's large frame, he crawled on his belly until he reached the far corner of the bed. Then he saw it, near the front passenger wheel, its pink rear end poking out from under a soiled pair of Spiderman under- wear. He grabbed the piggy and pulled it toward him, enjoy- ing the feel of the cool, smooth porcelain on his fingertips. He flipped it over, anxious to grasp the leafy contents inside.

As he started to pry open the underbelly he heard something . . . a giggle.

Surprised, he dropped his precious pig onto the carpet and held his breath. *Who was that?* He lay on his belly, too petrified to move. Another giggle—soft, sweet, melodic, and female.

He was desperately trying to figure out who it could be. The maid always finished work at 11:30 a.m.; otherwise he wouldn't have come home to raid his piggy bank. His parents were both supposed to be at work.

Then he heard her, laughing softly. It sounded like it was coming from the backyard. He got out from under his bed, leaving his piggy behind, and made his way over to the window, still open from the night before. He had forgotten to close it after he'd finished his last joint.

He stood at the window, looking left, looking right. He even looked up, hoping to find the source of the laughter, but saw no one. After several minutes, he heard nothing and figured his paranoia had gotten the better of him. Crawling back under the bed, he opened the pig's belly, and retrieved the pot.

Stepping over his dirty dishes, he made his way toward the hallway when he heard it again. It was the same laugh. This time it was louder and there was no mistake, it was coming from the backyard.

Curious, he made his way down the stairs, through the main foyer, past the luxurious dining room, and into the massive gourmet kitchen, toward the sunroom. His mother had insisted his father include a covered year-round sunroom off the kitchen in the house design to add an additional area for entertaining her friends. The sunroom had been designed by his mother and it was her own little piece of paradise.

When Evan heard another giggle, followed by his dad's voice, he stopped dead in his tracks. He moved quietly over to the kitchen window, so he could peer into the sunroom without being noticed. The room was flooded with light, piercing the designer windows his mom had chosen. It was a large, airy space with two indoor fireplaces, a dozen rounded chairs used as day beds, two swinging hammocks, a bar area, and a large television. It had been overdone to his mom's liking.

He didn't see them at first...one of the hammocks moved. They were snuggled in deep, wrapped in its netting like a caterpillar in its cocoon. They had left the door open; the only barrier: a screen.

He could hear everything they were saying. "Honey I'm addicted to you," his father professed in a deep sleepy tone—one he'd never heard his father use before. "I want you so badly."

Evan stopped breathing, taking in his father's words, and half expected the woman inside the hammock to take offence and jump out. Instead, she murmured, "I want you inside me. Now!"

The hammock moved and his father started to moan softly. The woman purred, "I've enjoyed you inside me in every room of this house, but I still prefer you in this hammock."

Evan's first instinct was to run outside the front door, past all the other massive houses littering their block until he reached the old oak tree near his school. As he was poised and ready to flee, something caught his eye. A glimpse of the woman's naked body peeking through the mesh stopped him dead in his tracks. Her perfectly formed nipple poked provocatively through the holes of the hammock. He instantly felt a welcome sensation between his legs.

His father started to move back and forth on top of her and she squealed, begging him for more. "Harder, baby. Harder," she pleaded.

Her words aroused Evan in a way he had never felt before and he watched as the outline of their bodies moved in unison. His father rode her briefly, moaning in ecstasy. He lay on top of her for a couple of minutes, then swung his body over the side of the hammock.

"Baby, stay with me," she cooed, sticking her leg out of the hammock, running her foot along his back.

His father's tone returned to normal. "You know our arrangement. No cuddling. Besides, my wife is coming home soon. Get your fine ass out of the hammock; we need to get going. I'll drive you home. We can swing by the bank. I owe for *two* cleaning jobs."

He winked at the woman, reached his hand into the hammock, and lifted her to her feet. Evan's mouth dropped several inches. He couldn't believe what he was seeing. It was the maid . . . the same maid who had cut his toe nails the previous week, the same maid who cleaned his room and made his bed. He was in shock!

With the hammock no longer impeding Evan's view he watched as she stood completely naked in his mother's sunroom, the sunlight emphasizing every inch of her luscious body. She was beautiful, head to toe. Her waist-length hair was silky black, her emerald eyes sparkled, and her skin was flawless.

He marveled at her and was suddenly happy his mother hired her last year as a favor to one of her tea friends. The friend's nineteen-year-old niece, who was taking night classes, cleaned homes during the day to help pay for her college degree. She'd been hoping to take on more jobs; she was hired.

Evan had never taken much of an an interest in women until he saw her—mostly because they wouldn't give him the time of day, but also because he had been too busy smoking pot. He was awkward and unattractive, spending most of his time alone. Seeing the maid awoke a newfound interest inside him.

Evan, a deer in the headlights, stood fixated on her breasts. He could have stared at them all afternoon, but suddenly he was startled from his trance hearing the zip of his father's pants. It was time to leave before he got caught. As he shifted position to move, he felt a wetness around his groin. Unknowingly, he'd ejaculated while watching the maid. He hid in the pantry—his father never deigned to cook, so he was safe there—until he heard them leave, raced upstairs to change his pants and underwear and effected his original exit plan, heading for the old oak tree.

Leaning against its coarse, woody trunk, enjoying the sooth-ing effects of the weed, his mind was still restless, hooked; all he could think about was the maid's naked body and he lusted for her. The remainder of the day was spent thinking about ways he could win her over, but each time his plan fell short as he knew she would never be attracted to him.

That night, he didn't sleep well and awoke feeling drained and tired. As he lay in bed, contemplating asking his mother to stay home sick, an idea came to him.

Bad Evan, he thought to himself. *Very bad Evan!*

Chapter 20
Very Bad Evan

EVAN WENT TO HIS BATHROOM, SPLASHED WATER on his face and around his armpits, then crawled back into bed and called for his mom. A few months earlier, he'd been sick and stayed home. His mom usually stayed with him, insisting, even at seventeen, his every need be taken care of, especially when he was sick.

She swept in, making a quick assessment; it was clear her baby was sick and suffering from a fever—he was sweating so badly. Knowing his mother would be busy at a local charity event, he suggested the maid as her replacement.

"What a wonderful idea, Honey. What ever made you think of her?" She kissed the top of his head and fussed with the sheets.

"It just came to me this morning." His smile was sly, already planning his attack.

The maid arrived to take care of him and started by cleaning up his room. He lay in bed watching her, wanting her badly. He had always viewed her as hired help, someone who tended to his every need, but this time he wanted her to service him in a much different way.

He continued to watch her as she bent over to pick up his dirty clothes, her breasts bulging out of her tight top. He could feel the sensation building up between his legs again and decided to implement his plan. He rang the bell his mom had placed on his bedside table, and the maid looked up and smiled. "How can I help?"

Boldly and eagerly, he commanded, "Service me like you do my father or I'm going to tell everyone about your affair." He knew she was well-respected in the community and was aspiring to become a physiotherapist. His plan had been to blackmail her into having sex with him.

She continued to smile, not skipping a beat. "Listen, hun, all you had to do was ask. I'll need you to share the contents of your piggy bank, though. I don't want the weed. I want the cash."

His mother gave him a weekly allowance of five hundred dollars, which he kept hidden with the weed. Obviously, the maid had been under his bed despite his threats! His stash wasn't as secret as he'd thought. The deal was fast and simple—they agreed on a sum of four hundred dollars a month. It ended up being a great deal for Evan because she looked after him weekly. It only cost him a hundred bucks per session. He even had money left over to buy weed.

She didn't mind charging less because his dad paid her very well, eight hundred a 'clean,' she had once told him. She worked for his family over the next four years until she finished university.

She not only kept the house spotless during those years but serviced Evan and his father. Evan's father never suspected he was sleeping with the maid. Fearing he would fire her if he knew, whenever his father was present, he bossed her around and treated her poorly.

Over the years, they became friends; she disclosed two other houses she 'cleaned.' It helped her pay for university. She referred to it as her own little side business. After the maid left, Evan was heart-broken and felt the experience had left him longing for unhealthy relationships.

* * *

As Samantha came to the end of the story hidden within Evan's journal, she showed pity for her husband. She reasoned it was his deceased father's fault for making him what he had become. Even though she tried to love him more after that night, giving him copious amounts of sex and attention, it obviously hadn't been enough.

My heart swelled at the realization of her situation. A woman who loved too much and a man who didn't love enough.

"Well, Samantha, we have two weeks. I'm certain I'll be able to gain his trust and get to the bottom of this." I filled my words with conviction and hope.

"Remember, he's a *very* private man," Samantha reminded me. "It may be harder than you think. He pays those women copious amounts of money to keep their mouths shut. If his mother ever found out, he'd be finished."

"Speaking of his mother, did she ever find out about the maid? Has she ever mentioned her to you?"

"I'd never heard about the maid. The next day, after I'd read his journal, I questioned him, asking if he'd ever had a maid. He became very upset and wanted to know why I was asking. I told him I was looking for some help around the house and figured with the size of his mother's home they must have had a maid. He bought my story but I let the subject drop, fearful he would find out I read his journal."

She sighed, looking deep in thought. I could almost see the wheels turning inside her head; the emotional turmoil a storm brewing inside. Her thoughts shifted suddenly. The winds of the storm taking another turn.

"Perhaps his grandmother had foreshadowed his frivolous ways at an early age, long before anyone else," Samantha grimaced. "Can you believe he still uses the piggy bank to this day? He stashes money in it all the time. It holds such fond memories for him. Every time he turns it over and takes the plastic rubber circle off, his eyes light up. Imagine!"

She shook her head in dismay. She was in the same situation Chloe had found herself in, wanting proof to ease her divorce. It was clear why Chloe had referred Samantha to me. Samantha got up to leave, tears rolling off her cheeks, shoulders hunched over, weighed down by her burdens. Still pretty, she looked much older than she did in her wedding photo; the stress of the marriage was aging her unkindly.

"You know what the sad thing is? I only found out he was cheating because I thought he was sick. After finding his medical folder stuffed with receipts I was worried he was dying. What a fool I turned out to be!"

Opening the motel room door, shaking her head in disbelief, she stepped into the darkness, disappearing into the night.

Chapter 21
Guns and Bibles

SAMANTHA, DISTRACTED BY HER GRIEF, LEFT without closing the door. The air was cool and a large draft managed to make its way into the room in the short time the door was left opened.

I shivered, closing the door, and grabbed a sweater from my suitcase, looking out the motel window, searching for Samantha, making sure she was safely in her car. A few minutes later, her car lights came on and I watched her drive off into the darkness. I yanked the curtains, making sure they were tightly shut, then scanned the room, looking for a work area, and deciding on a wooden chair nestled under a desk in the far corner of the room.

I sat down and opened the drawer in the middle of the desk, pleased to find what I was looking for—a piece of paper and a pen. I reached to the back, feeling around for more paper but instead my fingers landed on the edges of a book—*the Bible*. I'd never read it, but my beloved Uncle Rock had turned to it later in his life. I wondered, *Didn't Bibles go in the bedside table?*

I closed the wood drawer and poised the red pen in my hand, careful not to bring it to my mouth, a habit I'd had since elementary school, and began to make notes. I wanted to make sure I didn't forget anything Samantha had told me.

Evan didn't know me, so I'd planned to gain his interest using facts Samantha had disclosed. The information flowed easily from my pen.

I had wanted to add a few more items to the list but my pen ran out of ink. *Figures*, I thought, and aimed the pen toward the garbage sitting across the room. It hit the edge and landed inside the bin. Getting up, I stretched. It had been a long day and I was ready for bed.

The wind battered and rattled the windows, howling louder by the minute. A child cried a couple of doors down; the walls were as thin as the windows. The TV blared in the room next to mine, sending the sound of the gun shots through the walls.

Despite the cold and noise, I crawled into bed, dressed in double layers, hoping to get some rest. The long flight and Samantha's compelling story had taken their toll. Lying in bed, shivering, I cursed the cheap owner—who locked their thermostats at 66ºF?—and thought he and Evan would make great friends, the penny-pinching jerks. The numbers on the motel clock rolled over to 1:07 a.m. I eventually dozed off, only to be woken a short time later by sirens echoing in the distance.

A scream. *Someone in the corridor?* I jumped out of bed. Scared, I grabbed the wooden chair and shoved it under the door knob to add another level of protection between myself and the inhabitants of the dingy motel.

Satisfied my security measure was properly placed, I crawled under the covers again. The sheets were already cold from the short time I'd been out of bed. Wide awake again and trying to warm up, I curled my body into a ball, conserving heat. While waiting for exhaustion to take hold, I wondered, *Bree, what are you doing here?*

The lack of sleep was playing on my nerves and my surroundings only helped dampen my mood.

Another scream.

I jumped. More screams. More gun shots. I realized the sound was coming from the TV next door, not the corridor. My neighbor had increased his volume, *again.*

The sirens faded.

It took a long time to fall asleep. I'd already slept enough to trick my body into thinking it was rested. My primal instincts were on high alert. Convincing myself I was doing the cleaning staff a favor, I got up and moved the Bible to its proper place, the bedside table. I fell asleep with my hand resting on its crumpled cover, comforted, thinking of dear Uncle Rock.

Chapter 22
Let's Play Ball

I CHOSE AN INCONSPICUOUS SPOT ON A PARK BENCH near the ball diamonds to observe Evan from a distance. Despite my sleepless night, I was eager to finally get things started.

Samantha had told me he coached Little League baseball once a week and he loved it. He'd been a natural with the kids and they looked up to him. Originally, he'd taken on the task because his mother's friends were talking again. He'd lost his job the year before and he was still unemployed. She needed to dispel their gossip—volunteer work was her solution.

Evan was on the ball field, pointing this way and that, guiding the little bodies in different directions. He looked admirable as a coach and seemed to be enjoying himself. Jolly and round, he carried plenty of extra weight around his thighs and waist, and his belly moved while he talked. His jersey, two sizes too small, outlined his man boobs and showed the base of his belly, which hung over his belt. His lack of concern for his looks made him appear approachable and easy-going, which Samantha had assured me, the day before, was the case.

The practice ended and several children ran over to Evan, looking for a high five. One even gave him a hug before racing toward the play park nearby. Their grass-stained uniforms were in for another beating as they looked to expend whatever energy they had left. *Samantha was right,* I thought. *Not only does he love being a coach, but it appears the children love him equally as much. The smiling faces and high fives prove it!*

Evan moved to the side of the ball diamond and began talking to a strawberry blonde. He looked short standing beside her, although she looked out of place with her two-inch heels sinking into the turf. I didn't know of any women who wore heels to their eight-year-old son's baseball practice, but she was able to pull it off by complimenting her footwear with a dressed-down casual look: a snug tee and skinny jeans. With makeup, she looked to be about my age, but I suspected without the makeup and tight clothes, she was probably closer to ten years my senior. Her hair fell to her shoulders and she appeared relatively fit.

She was laughing, tossing her hair, touching his forearm, and tilting her head to one side. All the things I would have done when trying to bait a man. Evan was pointing to one of his players near home plate, the only boy who hadn't run off with the others. He resembled the woman Evan was talking to, so I assumed she was his mother.

He was swinging his bat through the air, pretending to hit a ball. He dropped his bat to the ground and looked far out into the field with his hand over his brow, shading his eyes from the sun. The boy suddenly jogged forward a few steps and waved toward the empty bleachers. He was pretending to have hit a home run.

As I waited for the conversation to end, I took the time to ponder the information I had on him. I was harsh with my review because I already wasn't fond of him. Samantha had painted a bleak picture of him, yet she still seemed to love him. He was cheating, unattractive, and sleazy—my final analysis. In my mind, this was even more evident watching him flirt openly, without reservation, with the boy's mom. Samantha had mentioned a few of the baseball moms often flirted with Evan because he'd then favor their sons, giving them more playing time and better field positions.

From the looks of it, this mom was working hard at getting her son a good one. He'd end up as pitcher or on first base for sure. It was plain to see Evan wanted to hit a 'home run' with her, but according to Samantha he'd never have an affair with one of the mothers. It'd be too risky. He didn't want to bring shame to his family name. Using hookers was safer because he paid for their silence. It was going to be tough to work my angle, with him being so cautious.

As I was contemplating how best to approach Evan, I noticed the boy had tired of his make-believe fans and was wandering away from his mother. She hadn't notice because she was too busy entertaining Evan by deliberately bending over in front of him while slowly picking up her son's baseball glove. She straightened, then turned to face him, with the glove in hand. They continued to talk, not growing weary of each other.

Evan appeared to be distracted by her cleavage. Her push up bra was doing its job . . . the magical bra men loved to hate. Luckily, I'd never needed this magic. My breasts held their own and were the perfect size, measuring just over a large handful, a generous C cup.

My breasts were not on display for the occasion. To entice him, I'd dyed my hair black, like the maid's, and tailored my look according to Samantha's suggestions: heels, a *very* fitted sundress, and ponytail. I wanted to be his every temptation, his every desire—his long-lost lover, the maid.

I was hoping my superficial 'innocent' look would appeal to Evan. After all, I'd learned he was partial to the naughty librarian look. I had bought a pair of fake glasses, which were poised and ready inside my purse just in case.

His interest in the cute strawberry blonde would have concerned me, but I was confident he wouldn't take the bait. As if he'd read my thoughts, he suddenly started to pack up the equipment littered around the field. She continued to follow him around, oblivious to the fact he was getting ready to leave.

I shifted on the bench, reached for my purse, and dabbed a touch of powder to my nose, looking at the reflection in the small compact mirror. I was ready to pounce.

Samantha and I had agreed the best place to approach him was after baseball, but I still hadn't decided on the most natural and unsuspecting way to introduce myself. My cover story was going to be this: I was temporarily house sitting for a friend and I was in college, looking for a volunteer experience to spend my free time while I was in town. As for the rest, I wasn't sure . . . I was going to make it up as I went.

I stood up and adjusted my dress, looking around to determine the best angle for my approach. I knew it was going to be difficult to convince him I wasn't a threat and could be trusted. It wasn't often a pretty stranger just randomly wanted to volunteer, but I was hoping he'd bite, thinking I was doing it for my resume and future job aspirations. I needed to be on my best game to pull this off.

I started to over think my approach, and my overabundance of confidence was being replaced with doubts. I was considering postponing our first encounter, thinking, *perhaps I should just watch him for today*, when I noticed the boy near a store. I, too, distracted with Evan like his mother, lost track of his whereabouts and he had wandered off to a nearby candy store.

The store was charming with its pink shutters and bright orange door. The exterior looked like it had been splattered with paint and an assortment of pastel colors presented themselves on the bricks. The massive windows displayed a multitude of candy, which had enticed the spirited boy. It was a parent's nightmare, but a dentist and child's dream. The candy beckoned children to enter, just as Hansel and Gretel had been lured into the witch's house.

From the park bench, I watched the boy enter the store. The windows were large enough I could see inside; he was standing by the front counter, near a flashing neon light advertising the sale of soft ice cream. He did not appear concerned he was alone; instead, he looked at ease, with his head held high; enjoying his freedom. I suspected it wasn't the first time he'd wandered off. He was likely accustomed to his mother's attention being elsewhere.

Evan picked up the last of the baseball equipment and pointed at his watch. It was no longer a hint but a definite cue now. The woman started looking around for her son. She turned around, making a full 360-degree turn, looking in every direction. Her smile faded, and concern immediately washed over her face. "Timmy? Timmy, where are you?"

As quickly as her heels would allow, she wobbled over to the adjacent park, looking for him there. Nothing. She yelled his name, the panic evident in her voice. Evan, too, looked concerned and asked the boy's teammates if they had seen him.

I was already making my way over to the store. I had an idea and was seizing the opportunity.

Chapter 23
Piggly the Pig

A CHIME EMITTED A SOFT RING AS I ENTERED THE store. A small elderly female, who I assumed was the owner, nodded and smiled, and I returned the gesture. Timmy didn't look up. He had moved on from the chocolate bars he'd been examining and was now hypnotized by a large sucker roughly the size of his head.

I walked around the store, looking for something the boy might like as I waited for Evan and Timmy's mom to figure out he'd made his way over to the convenience store. The choices were limitless, and I was overwhelmed by the amount of candy the owner had managed to stuff on the shelves.

I was about to choose a container of gummies when I saw exactly what I needed on the highest shelf in the store, a piggy bank! I picked it off the top shelf and dusted it off. The little old lady, vertically challenged, had most likely been unable to reach the shelf because of her short stature, and the items had accumulated dust.

The piggy bank was cute, about the size of my hand. The flamboyant label around its belly advertised him as

"Piggly the pig." According to its vibrant lettering, the pig contained chocolate coins.

Perfect!

I stood beside the cash register, piggy bank in hand, waiting for service and observing Timmy as he moved over to another shelf with infinite amounts of colorful packages.

The owner was waiting to take my money. She nodded her head instead of engaging in conversation and pointed to the total on the register, $10.24. As I reached into my purse for some cash, I could see Evan and Timmy's mom heading toward the store. I quickly paid and knelt beside Timmy, bringing myself to his height. "Hey, kiddo. Do you like chocolate?" Smiling. I showed him the piggy bank.

He furrowed his brows and crossed his arms. "I don't take chocolate from strangers."

His defiant response made me smile from ear to ear. "Well, aren't you a smart little man."

"I'm not little," he retorted, giving additional attitude. The kid had taken his wings of independence seriously. He was assertive and cute all at the same time.

"Well, maybe we can ask your mom if you can have it?"

"My mom?" He paused, considering my proposal. "Sure, she's outside. Let's go."

He grabbed my hand and pulled me toward the doorway. He was surprisingly strong. We stepped out onto the sidewalk and were blinded by the sun. He steered me toward the park, determined to have the piggy bank as a gift.

His mom started to cry at the sight of him and took him in her arms. Evan was staring at me, his mouth slightly ajar. He was obviously impressed. As Timmy's mom showered affection on her son, Evan's eyes shifted downwards, checking out my delights. He took notice of the piggy bank in my right hand and I could see a look of amusement on his face. Timmy's mom straightened up and held her son's hand tightly.

I introduced myself. "Hi, I'm Bree." I had decided not to change my name to avoid any slip-ups. "I noticed your son was alone in the store and I wanted to make sure he wasn't lost, so we came out to find you. He is a smart young man. He wouldn't take chocolate from me unless you approved it. So, if it's OK with you, can he have this?" I held out the piggy bank and the chocolate coins rattled inside.

Before answering, she looked at me from top to bottom then looked at Evan, his droopy eyes, half-smile, and slack-jaw giving away his thoughts. If he didn't close his mouth soon, drool was certain to escape the corner of it at any time.

"No!" she barked disapprovingly at me instead of her son. "He's not allowed to have it. He ran off without telling me. No rewards for bad behavior."

I had to give her that. It sounded reasonable. I looked at Timmy, who was about to cry. "Sorry, Bud, but your mom is right."

"No, she isn't." He looked at his mother with complete disgust. He was crying and stamping his feet in protest.

"Evan, I'm walking Timmy to the car. Are you joining us?" Her words clipped and sharp, not expecting a refusal; he disappointed her.

"No," he rebuffed, not taking his eyes off me. "I'm going to stay and chat with this lovely lady. I'll see you at next week's practice."

"Uh . . . fine, then," she stammered before she and Timmy stomped off toward the parking lot, Timmy angry about the piggy bank and his mom about the coach's lack of attention.

"Hello, beautiful. I'm Evan," he spoke in a sexy voice that didn't match his physical appearance. "Are you new in town? I haven't noticed you around before."

"You're too kind," I quipped, looking toward the ground, twirling the ends of my ponytail, and pretending to be bashful. "I'm in town for a couple of weeks, house sitting for a friend. He's in Taiwan on business. I'm in college nearby, so I agreed. How about you? Do you live in town? I see you play baseball."

I pointed to the baseball glove he was carrying. His eyes followed my every move. For added playfulness, I laced strands of my newly dyed hair between my fingers, tugging gently at the tips.

He stood closer to me and inhaled, breathing in the smell of my vanilla perfume. He was clearly already enamored with me. "I live in town. I like to volunteer and coach the local baseball team. The boy you were helping is on my team. That was very kind of you, by the way."

"He was alone. I just wanted to make sure he had a parent nearby. It was no problem at all." I moved closer and brushed myself against his arm, then whispered into his ear, "And besides, it gave me the opportunity to meet you."

He looked at me with hungry eyes. "I'm happy to have met you too. If there's anything I can do to facilitate your stay, I'd be more than happy to help out."

I put my finger to my lips, nibbling on the tip as I pretended to think of something he could do for me, then I touched his arm. "As chance would have it, I need volunteer hours. My college insists its students become *active* in their communities so, maybe I could help you coach over the next two weeks? I'm not a fan of kids, but I need the hours." I was looking at him with large doe eyes, pleadingly.

"I'd enjoy having you." He winked, and I caught the double intent behind his words. He was already making an inference he wanted to sleep with me. Things were rolling along well, but would I be able to take him to the next level, beyond flirtation?

I ran my hands along the sides of my body, tracing out my curves, looking at the ground shyly, basking in his attention. I wanted him to believe I was a naughty librarian type, shy but willing.

"Do you have any children on the team? Are you married?" I kept playing with my hair, keeping my eyes lowered.

"I've got three children, but they are all too young to join sports teams. I'm recently divorced, but like to help out when I can."

Ohh . . . he lied about his marital status, giving the perception of being single.

"I'd enjoy your company and some extra help with coaching over the next two weeks." Unable to keep the lust out of his eyes, he measured me up once again. "Can I call you tomorrow with details?"

"That would be great." I squeezed his arm to show my gratitude.

He closed his eyes and sucked in a deep breath, enjoying my touch.

"Wow, do you work out? You have great definition in your forearms." Another thing off the list from the night before. Samantha had mentioned her husband believed his best feature was his arms, so I complimented him, despite the fact his arm felt flabby.

"I have been known to work out from time to time." He chuckled, his belly reminding me of a bowl of jelly.

"Maybe we could *hook up* sometime and workout." I made eye contact with him, my eyes piercing his, knowing he would get the double meaning.

"I'd love to *hook up* with you." He slid his hand over my bottom, looking around for witnesses as he did. We were alone; he was safe, the baseball crowd having left over an hour ago.

"I'm parked over there. Wanna walk me to my car?" I grinned, pulling him in nearer, pointing to the parking lot across the street. I had purposely parked near Evan's truck, prepared.

"Sure, lead the way."

Guiding my catch to the car, I leaned up against it. Out of breath from the short walk, Evan did the same. I waited for him to catch his breath, then grabbed his baseball jersey, drawing him closer.

"I want you to have this." I handed him the piggy bank, knowing the sentimental value it held. "I'd bought it for Timmy, but since he couldn't have it, I'd like you to have it. A little souvenir of our evening." I was trying to tap into his deep-seated desires by jogging his memory.

He shook his head in utter disbelief. "You have no idea how much this piggy bank brings back special memories for me. Thank you."

I almost felt sorry for him, playing with his emotions, until he continued with a coy smile. "Actually," he said, tracing his finger along the nape of my neck, "you remind me of someone special, someone I have *very* fond memories of, a lady who used to work for my family, our maid. She treated me very . . . very well."

Grinning shrewdly, likely relishing memories of their sexual adventures, he massaged the back of my neck.

"Do you like little maids? Dirty ones?" I asked, my voice sexy, lips pouting.

He gawked in complete lust and adoration. His cheeks turned crimson red at my words. Seizing the opportunity, I pulled him in closer, pushing my body into his. I boldly ran my hand along his hardness. He didn't even flinch.

I purred into his ear. "I need volunteer hours, but I also do a little work on the side to make extra cash to help pay for college."

He pulled away, looking shocked.

I scolded myself. *Why did I move so quickly?* I'd been warned he was private.

"Wow! You are *exactly* like her."

"Like the maid?" I played innocent, happy his shock was attributed to my similarities with the past lover, not my sexual aggression. If he only knew his wife had told me the whole story.

"I want you so badly. You're stunning. You bring back so many memories for me. How much?"

As we started to bargain, I reached into my purse and pressed the record button on my phone.

"One thousand for the complete package," I demanded with conviction, using the figure Samantha had provided as a reference point. I fondled his hardness. "I'll do whatever you want but condoms are non-negotiable." My stomach queasy, I focused on the soft, silky material of his shorts.

Moaning in the crook of my neck, he brought his hand downward, grabbing at my breasts, roughly massaging them. "Eight hundred with a condom or I'll give you twelve hundred to go bareback." Clearly he was an excellent negotiator.

I countered, stroking him a little harder, "Nine hundred with condom. It's non-negotiable."

His breathing increased, seemingly ready to cum.

Time to cool things off.

"No more 'til I see some cash." I gently pushed him away. "Consider it a preview of my services."

He sighed, disapprovingly.

I reeled him back in; a fish on a hook. "Why don't we just go back to your place? You're divorced right?"

"Yes, but the kids are home, so we can't. We could always go back to your friend's house?" He raised an eyebrow questionably.

"No," I protested, maybe a little too abruptly. Recovering, I fabricated a story about my friend's nosey neighbors, the pieces fitting together easily for me; I was a little surprised I was already becoming proficient at lying.

"I wasn't sure I wanted to deal with you until you showed such an overt concern for wanting to keep this transaction private."

"Listen, Evan, I only do this a handful of times throughout the school year to help pay for my tuition. I enjoy it but don't plan to make it a habit. I don't want anyone to find out my extra-curricular activities. Let's keep this discreet." My voice stern, hands placed on either hip, I resembled a teacher scolding her students.

"I like the way you think, beautiful. I have a guest house we could use." I knew he was referring to his mother's guest house, the one he'd lived in during his bachelor days. He cupped his hand around my crotch and I wanted to vomit, but smiled instead.

Lightly pushing his hand away, I whispered into his ear, "I told you, money first."

Opening the door, I got into my rental car and rolled down the window. He pushed his groin inside my open window. "Bet you can't wait to have a taste of this."

Licking my lips, I leaned toward the large tent jutting from his shorts; he was obviously very well endowed. "I'm going to have it all night long baby," I teased.

He reached inside his shorts and started to move his hand up and down his shaft. I knew it was best to join in, wanting to make my involvement believable, so I started placing my hands over my breasts, fondling them while his erection danced in front of my face. I preferred it this way, my hands instead of his. He was moaning and moving his hand faster, readying himself yet again. The sound of a car in the distance…saved…he quickly withdrew.

"Shit, I wanted to cum so badly," he complained as he withdrew his hand from his shorts and moved away from my car. He knelt so I could see his chubby face, flushed from the excitement. "I'll call you soon. Maybe even tonight. I have a few things I want to put in order before we get started." His breath stank of garlic and I wanted to turn away and gag.

I'm sure you do, I thought, *like finding an excuse to get out of the house.*

He playfully tapped the side of my car door. "Hey, by the way, do I get a discount if I sign off on your volunteer hours without you having to set foot on the field?"

I laughed, thinking he was joking. He wasn't. He was probably the cheapest person I'd ever met, but he had a point. "OK, we'll make it eight hundred even and I don't have to hang out with a bunch of kids. That's worth at least a hundred."

He nodded in agreement, took down my number, then climbed into his truck and sped out of the parking lot, squealing his tires, trying to impress me. I clicked off the record button and dialed Samantha's number. Things couldn't have worked out better.

Chapter 24
Hook, Line, and Sinker

SAMANTHA ANSWERED AFTER THE FIFTH RING. SHE'D been putting the kids to bed and had left her phone in the kitchen after working on the dishes, so she hadn't heard the first few rings. Her activities were a stark contrast to her husband's, eliciting sex from a stranger. *Unbelievable.*

"Did you get a chance to talk to him? I'm sure he noticed you."

She sounded exhausted; it was already past nine and she had been running after three young kids all evening. I could hear water running in the background, likely from her finishing the dishes.

"Actually, he'll be home soon and looking for an excuse to leave the house again. He's planning to take me to the guest house tonight. I got the whole thing recorded on my phone!" I'd wanted to break the news to her softly, but it was almost impossible under the circumstances.

She gasped as glass broke in the background. "Shit!"

"What happened?"

"I was washing his favorite coffee mug. Pissed—I smashed it on the counter and cut my finger."

"Can I do anything?" I knew my offer was pointless, but I wasn't sure what else to say.

"You've done plenty," she said, her voice flat.

"I'm sorry to have upset you. I saw an opportunity and went for it. I know this is hard but—"

Samantha interrupted me. "I'm not mad at you, my dear. I'm disgusted and upset with that lowlife piece of crap. You did an excellent job. I'm proud of you. He's so stupid and determined to sleep with you, he forgot about his mother's security cameras. Now we can get video too."

It was my turn to be surprised! "Security cameras? Do we need them? I recorded my conversation with him. He offered me money for sex. Do you really need more proof?" I exclaimed, not liking where she was headed.

"Bree, this is the perfect opportunity to catch him in the act. He'll deny he was ever going to sleep with you. This way we have him hook, line, and sinker."

"How will you be able to record us? It's his mom's place. It will never work." I retorted, trying to head her off at the pass.

"I have complete access to her security system. She was busy at one of her charity events last year and had asked me to stay over while a contractor set up her cameras. She had them installed all over the property, even inside the guest house. There are no cameras inside the bedroom, obviously, but she did have one installed in the main living area. The cameras are tiny, almost impossible to see. I do the up-keep on the security system. She knows nothing about electronics.

"Shit, the front door just opened. He's here!" Her voice fell to a whisper. "Get him into the living room and I'll take care of the rest. The idiot couldn't have picked a better spot. Bye and good luck," she said casually, as though I were studying for an important test or interviewing for a new job.

Tossing my phone onto the passenger seat, I exhaled, discouraged my audio recording wasn't enough to satisfy her. She wanted more, but I couldn't blame her. He'd plead his case to his mother, saying it was a weak moment, and he'd never intended to follow through. His mom would cave, wanting to believe the best of her baby.

It was going to be difficult, but I was up for the challenge. I just hoped my stomach would hold out.

Chapter 25
Be my guest

EVAN CALLED AN HOUR LATER. "I'M IN MY TRUCK going to get some condoms. I found a sitter. I can swing by and pick you up."

Funny he never mentioned the sitter was his wife. "I'd rather meet you. I'll take a cab. I'm not fond of driving at night."

"That'd work." He gave me the address to the guest house. We agreed to rendezvous in an hour.

Samantha had called ten minutes earlier, after he left the house. He had started a fight over his broken coffee mug and stormed out—the perfect excuse to leave. According to Samantha, Evan's mom wasn't set to come home until early the next morning. By the time his mother arrived, my mission would be complete, and I'd be long gone. *"What will his mother do once she finds out he's been using her money to pay for hookers?"* I mused.

Fifty–five minutes later, my cab pulled up outside his mother's very large estate. I paid the cabbie and stood on the driveway, admiring the large home. The house was luxurious and extremely well-maintained, but every section of the home looked homogeneous and sterile.

Keeping with the naughty librarian look Evan liked so much, I'd pinned my dark hair up in a loose bun, with strands falling to the sides. I wore my thinned framed fake glasses and had chosen a black knee-length jacket to cover the purple lace peek-a-boo negligée I had on underneath. I was planning to spend as little time as possible with Evan, hoping he would cream himself at the very sight of me. According to Samantha, he didn't last very long in bed, evident in the parking lot earlier. He seemed easily excitable.

I was hoping to be back to the motel within the hour, preferring it over him—which was saying a lot. I adjusted my jacket and headed to the front door when I heard a car door open.

Startled, I looked around, catching a glimpse of a truck. The driveway was dimly lit and the only light I had to work with came from the street lights behind me.

"Come over here, sexy." It was Evan, his voice clear. The cab was unlit, obscuring him, I could barely make him out.

I sauntered over to his vehicle, looking sexy yet saucy, my large hoop earrings brushing against my cheeks as I tilted my head to get a better look. Evan was dressed in black, but his pale skin gave him away. He patted the passenger seat, motioning me inside. "Jump in. I've been thinking about how much I'd like to pound you right here… in my truck."

Although alarmed by his vulgar words, I managed to stay calm. I smiled and took it in stride while I frantically looked for an excuse to get him to the guest house. No way

I wanted to be trapped inside the close quarters of his truck. *His truck! That was my out!*

"My dad has the exact same model and color of truck. I—" My voice held the perfect mix of disgust and lust. I shook my head. "I'm sorry, babe, but it'd absolutely ruin the mood for me."

My excuse was met with disdain. The smug smile on his face changed to anger. "I'm paying you a lot of money and I don't care if you're a little uncomfortable. I want to have you inside this truck." He slapped the passenger seat for effect.

The gall of this man! I wanted nothing more than to tell him off . . . but I had to catch the creep red-handed. Knowing he liked dirty talk, I used my silkiest voice. "Believe me honey, I'll be able to taste you a lot better in bed." He was smirking now. "I'm 100 percent sure you will be satisfied with my performance. If you aren't, I'll let you have me a second time in the truck at no charge."

"How can I say no to such an offer? You drive a hard bargain."

Appealing to his cheap, perverted side had won him over quickly. His large belly in the way, he exited the truck with some difficulty, and waddled toward the backyard in anticipation. The night had cooled off a few more degrees and a cold draft ran up my jacket; I wrapped it tightly around my waist. It was early fall and the days were warm, but the evenings cool.

The backyard was immaculate. The gardener had done a magnificent job of maintaining the yard and the pool. The pool lights were on and steam rose from the water. The pool was heated, and the warmth escaped into the night. The guest house was set toward the back of the yard. It looked like a beach house off the cover of a luxury magazine. No wonder Evan had never wanted to move out. I would have wanted to stay, too, if the circumstances were different.

Evan had managed to scurry ahead of me, like a weasel— a fat weasel—in the dark. He reached the opulent entrance of the guest house, and his stout fingers fumbled with the keys, anxious for his sexual favors, and unlocked the large brown door.

"In here." He motioned me inside. He was whispering and out of breath again from the short walk. A bead of sweat fell from his brow and his sparse greasy hair looked moist. No one was around but he was being careful nonetheless. Quickening my pace, I stepped through the doorway, welcoming the heat. He shut the door quickly and locked it. Without a word, he moved around the room, shutting the blinds while I stood just inside the doorway. As the last blinds fell shut with a thud, he turned on the lights.

The main room was tastefully decorated to look like a sports bar. It had a man cave look with pizzazz. It was meant to favor a man's taste; nevertheless, it had a subtle female touch and even smelled of lavender.

Evan made his way over to the sleek leather couch and reached into his jacket pocket, pulling out a large stack of folded bills. He brought the money to his nose and inhaled. "I'm not sure what I like more—the smell of money or women." He flapped the money around his groin, beckoning me over like a dog for a treat.

Clearly, he liked having the upper hand and money made him feel powerful. He was used to these types of business transactions and was enjoying himself. Money and sex were his weaknesses, but he viewed them as his strengths.

"Do you want to count it?" He sat down and laid the money on his groin. I shook my head. "Why so shy? Come join me on the couch. Take off your jacket and stay awhile." He chuckled at this provocation and spread his legs wider, snapping his fingers as he did, and pointed to the bulge in his pants.

Nervously, I shook my head again. "I trust you. I don't need to count it."

I was shaking, more apprehensive than cold. "Baby, I need to freshen up a little for you. Why rush? Let's put on some music and take our time." I was having cold feet and needed a quiet place to refocus.

"You look just fine! Besides, you're shaking. Let me warm you up." He placed the money on the coffee table and started to unzip his pants.

"I need to use the ladies' room," I pleaded, dancing around a little, like I had to pee.

"Second door to the left." He pointed toward the back of the house, looking annoyed. I flashed him a sexy smile, but he didn't notice. He was already struggling to take off his pants.

I slipped past him, heading for the bathroom. His directions were accurate, and I found it within seconds. I closed the door and locked it, creating an additional barrier between us. The bathroom was as ritzy as the rest of the house. It had double sinks, a large glass shower, and a Jacuzzi tub.

I was feeling faint and grasped the sides of one of the sinks. Looking at myself in the mirror, I breathed deeply. My chest walls heaved as I inhaled in and slowly exhaled out. "You can do this! You can do this!" I repeated it to myself over and over until my body relaxed and the tension between my shoulder blades released. I wanted to catch him and knew I could—but having to get physical with someone repugnant—was a whole different story. Maybe if he had been as gorgeous as Chloe's husband it would have been easier to stomach. Giggling, I thought, *I should have asked for more money!* Making light of the situation gave me a renewed strength.

My motivational pep talk managed to warm me. I removed my glasses, securing them inside my coat pocket and hung the coat over the tub. Looking down, I noticed my negligée needed some adjusting. I fussed with the straps and portions of the material, managing to tweak the lace so it hugged all the right places.

My breasts were spilling out of my bra, which was one size too small. Samantha had suggested the purple lace because it was Evan's favorite. I wore a matching thong panty, which showed off my toned buttocks.

Music started playing in the background. It sounded like hard rock. Choosing this genre of music meant only one thing . . . aggressive sex.

One last check in the mirror. I looked stunning; it wouldn't take him long.

I made my way back to the living room, slowly turning the corner, trying to delay, and with good reason: I was greeted by Evan's naked body, every ounce of him on display. He was sprawled out on the couch. My eyes went straight to his large belly. It was ghostly white and lumpy. His appendage, barely visible, hidden by the fat, was poking out from the side. It reminded me of a white bun hiding a wiener.

"Gorgeous! Absolutely heavenly!" He sighed under his breath. "You look so much like her. This is going to be the best day of my life . . . since I had her last." He smacked his lips, anticipating what was about to come.

"I'm glad you're pleased." I curtsied, and he applauded.

He rolled to one side, easing his large body off the couch. The hair on the back of my neck stood up. This was going to be more difficult than I'd originally thought. After he managed to get himself off the couch, he waddled over, his short chubby legs moving as quickly as they could. His pudgy hands were around my waist and on my breasts within seconds.

I gasped as he pushed his lips on mine and forced his tongue down my throat. He was an awful kisser and his breath still reeked of garlic. I wanted to vomit. I closed my eyes; unsuccessfully envisioning Adam in front of me, as Evan continued to grope at my breasts and undo the clasp of my undersized B cup bra. My breasts spilled out, exposing themselves for his full viewing pleasure.

"Those are some big firm tits you have." He nodded in approval, filling both of his hands with my breasts and shoving his face between them. He started licking and tonguing my nipples. His tongue was fast and skilled. He was much better with his tongue on my nipples then he had been in my mouth. His proficiency, never the less, was still repulsive.

I had no intention of sleeping with him. I'd do what was necessary to get the proof Samantha needed to divorce his cheating ass. My blood was boiling, making it increasingly difficult to stay.

He enjoyed the fullness of my breasts for several minutes before taking my hand and placing it between his legs. Wrapping my fingers around his hardness, I could feel his large girth. Curiosity got the best of me. Forcing my eyes open, I marveled at his size. He had the most perfect organ I had ever seen. If only it were attached to a better body! Evan looked satisfied with my reaction.

"Jasper's a good size, isn't he?"

His appendage had a name! I couldn't believe it. And . . . Jasper? I wanted to ask but didn't.

"The biggest I've ever seen!" I gasped, my eyes wide, playing the part, flattering his large ego. Truth be told, he was big, I gave him that. I reluctantly stroked him over and over, hoping he would climax quickly, but it seemed he had got used to a woman's touch and it was taking longer than anticipated. He'd been willing to peak easily in the parking lot only a few hours earlier. *Had he taken a little blue pill for the occasion?*

He suddenly grabbed my sex, roughly, handling it like hamburger meat being mixed for a patty. Pain radiated from between my legs and I instinctively backed away. He flinched, noticeably disturbed by my reaction.

"Enough of this touchy stuff. I'm ready to take it to the next level." He pulled me into him again and guided me downwards.

Giving him oral sex was out of the question. Besides, I'd probably vomit. I had discussed my comfort level with Samantha before she hired me. No full-blown sexual acts, but I let him guide me to my knees, continuing to caress his fullness. He tossed his head back, moaning in delight.

I artfully played with the tip and lightly pinched it between my fingers. Running my hands along the side of his sex, I gently squeezed, making the veins turn a deeper purple. He continued to enjoy the touch of my hands for several minutes, but I knew it wouldn't last for long. Most men craved a woman's lips rather than her hands. Indeed, he soon grew impatient. Grabbing the back of my hair, he forced my face into his groin. "Take it," he commanded. "I wanna see if you can handle Jasper."

I pushed my head back, resisting.

"What's wrong? Jasper too big for ya?" Throwing his head back, he roared, his stomach jiggling from the hearty laugh.

The rock music thumped in the background, matching the pounding in my head. I was feeling faint again. I couldn't put up with his tactics much longer.

He forced my head into his groin once more. "Just have a little taste. Then I'll ride you like the other women. They love it."

Then I heard it—the sweet sound I'd been waiting for; his phone rang, startling him.

I looked up, smiling, knowing he was finally defeated. Grabbing his appendage and ball sack as tight as I could, I squeezed as if I were juicing a lemon.

He grimaced and yelled out in pain as he fell backward onto the floor. Getting to my feet, I stood over him. He looked as pathetic as he was, curling himself into a ball, moaning in pain.

"The phone's for you. Your wife's calling."

Samantha had remotely activated his mom's security system from her cell phone and was videotaping our session. Before I'd arrived, we'd agreed she would call his phone once she was satisfied she had enough proof.

We had achieved our goal: he was naked in his mother's guest house, caught on tape trying to have sex with me and he'd even admitted to having sex with other women. Case closed!

I retrieved my jacket from the bathroom and returned to the living room, grabbing the money from the table as I headed toward the door.

He was struggling to get up, rage on his face. "You stupid bitch. I'm going to—"

I cut him off. "What are you going to do, Evan? Call your *mommy*? Do you really think she'll be happy to hear you used her guest house and money to hire me? What would her little tea ladies think?"

The shock and confusion on his face was priceless. The irony and sarcasm of my questions made him flinch and he crumpled to the floor, holding his injured groin with one hand and his head with the other, trying to figure out what had just happened.

Now, it was my turn to be angry. "You're disgraceful and don't deserve the beautiful family you have." I flung the door open and turned to face him. "By the way, say hi to the camera!" I waved toward the camera hidden near the television and slammed the door shut.

Like a determined soldier in the midst of battle, I marched all the way to the front of the house, livid and repulsed with the whole situation, eager for a hot shower to wash his stench off my body. Stuffing his money in my coat pocket with one hand, I withdrew my phone with the other, sending a request for a driver. The app signaled a five-minute arrival time. I paced along the sidewalk, waiting impatiently. My fury kept me warm.

Luckily, the driver pulled up a minute early. Evan, now furious, came hurtling out from the backyard with the camera dangling from his hand. He'd ripped it out of the wall.

I escaped into the cab and saucily waved at him as he stood in the middle of the roadway, defeated. As the cab rounded the bend, Evan threw the camera onto the pavement, stomping it. I settled back into my seat. *Mission accomplished.*

Chapter 26
On the Road Again

ON THE SHORT CAB RIDE BACK TO THE MOTEL, I thought about Samantha. Was she secretly happy to have finally caught him, or was she stricken with grief? Probably a bit of both, I suspected. Regardless, the deal was done, the truth was out, the choice was hers.

On arrival, I requested the driver wait, telling him I'd be maybe half an hour. Leaping out of the cab, I ran up the steps to my room. I quickly removed my negligée and tossed it in the trash. As I showered, the filth made its way into the drain, cleansing both my physical and emotional self. I gladly changed into jeans and a t-shirt. Packing in haste, I threw my toothbrush and makeup into my pink suitcase and zipped it closed. Fearful of the unkempt room, I'd kept most of my belongings packed.

I needed to create some distance. Evan didn't know where I was staying but Samantha did. I trusted her not to say anything, but perhaps she had left a paper trail, as Evan had done with his hookers, and I didn't want to take any chances he'd find me.

Taking one last look around the room for any forgotten items, I opened the bedside table and noticed the Bible. Running my fingers along its broken cover, I smiled. "Thanks," I whispered, under my breath, appreciating the comfort it had provided the night before. I closed the drawer, grabbed my suitcase off the grungy bed, and darted down the steps to check out.

The same receptionist was at the front desk. It looked like she hadn't left since I'd arrived; she was wearing the same washed-out clothes and had the same '80s hairdo. I handed her cash. She wasn't surprised. This type of business was used to cash deals and she didn't ask any questions. I'd booked for two weeks and was paying in full, so she didn't care. She was happy. She could rent the room again for the rest of the time and make double the money for her thrifty boss, or—who knew—maybe she pocketed it for herself. After she'd counted the fourteen Benjamin Franklins, wetting her yellow-stained finger tips before flipping each bill, she mumbled thanks and forced a half-smile.

Before long, I was back in the cab. The driver had only waited twenty minutes according to the meter. On the road again, I was relieved to be heading for the airport. Using the same MO, I was heading straight home; just as I'd done with Chloe.

The ride to the airport passed quickly. The driver wasn't comfortable speaking English so there was little dialogue between us. The peace and quiet was appreciated. My headache had gotten worse, my temples thumped, a pounding throbbing pain—there was no room for small talk. We pulled up to the airport departures terminal and I reached into my pocket for my credit card, to realize I was wearing the same coat I'd worn to see Evan. His eight hundred dollars was still in my pocket. I'd forgotten all about it. The driver's mouth formed into the shape of an O, surprised to see the wad of cash I had just pulled out of my pocket. He was even more surprised when I handed it all to him.

"What?" he inquired in a thick accent, looking panicky. His eyes were large with shock.

"For your family." I gestured to the photo taped to his dashboard showing off his wife and five children. I didn't want any of Evan's filthy money. I'd only taken it out of disgust because I knew how much he loved it.

The driver protested and pushed the money back in my direction, making me want him to have it even more.

"I insist!" I said forcefully. "For your children."

He hesitated, then bowed his head graciously, accepting the money. "For my children."

He stuffed the money into his jacket pocket, looking overwhelmed; we moved to the rear of his cab to remove my suitcase from the trunk. He took it out quickly and set it on the ground, extending the handle while passing it to me.

I held out my hand, intending to shake his before I left. It seemed appropriate for the occasion. After all, I'd just given him eight hundred dollars!

Instead, he gave me a quick hug and darted back inside the cab. I suspected he was overcome with emotion by my generosity; a handshake would not suffice. I appreciated his kind gesture as he had appreciated mine.

Four hours later, I boarded the plane, happy to be going home. While waiting for the flight, I had received several messages from Samantha. Evan had come home right away—knowing the gig was up—he confessed. Samantha figured everything was fine; they had already managed to discuss the terms of their separation. She agreed not to tell his mother about the hookers; he agreed to shred the prenuptial. She hadn't even asked!

Another happy ending, I thought as I ordered a glass of red wine. Taking a long, rewarding sip, I applauded myself aloud, "Cheers on a job well done!"

An attentive passenger beside me looked over with a smirk on his face, likely thinking I was drunk because I was talking to myself. "Congrats!" he acquiesced.

I nodded at him then lifted my glass and took another long sip.

The stranger wanted to chat, but I politely declined, choosing my earphones as company. Some classical music was in order. Closing my eyes, I sipped the wine, and thought of Samantha . . . not Evan. Luckily, the alcohol was allowing me to suppress those memories. Knowing she already had things under control; it helped validate what I was doing.

The plane touched down a few hours later and I felt energized. I'd helped another couple come to terms with the reality of their marriage. I was sure lady Karma was pleased. Personally, I'd come to terms with being a mistress for hire. . . and was already contemplating doing it again!

Chapter 27
Eeny, Meeny, Miny, Moe

ENJOYING THE THIRD WEEK OF MY VACATION, IN A cozy bed and breakfast nestled inside the city of Versailles, I pondered the last few days of my journey while sipping a cappuccino. After returning from Nevada and dealing with Evan, I was spoiling myself after a job well done. I'd stopped by the Chic Chick before leaving, bottle of rum in hand and gave my notice. Josh and the owner were sad to see me go—saying, "You'll always have a spot if you change your mind."

Always wanting to see Europe but never having the time or money, I now had both. I'd booked the first flight to Europe, hoping to discover some of it's wonders, starting with Belgium and now on the last leg of the trip in France. The trip had been a success. I'd seen many breath-taking sights, met several interesting people. But it was ending—word was spreading fast; clients were looking for my help.

Taking the last sip of my hot beverage, my thoughts turned to my mission; I wanted to continue to make things right, perhaps even subconsciously trying to buy myself a

ABBY PARKER

place beside Uncle Rock. I wasn't sure, but what I did know was this: Karma had kicked my butt . . . being a mistress cheated on by another mistress, and I deserved it! Now, I was rectifying my past, providing solace to wives contending with the kind of woman I used to be. And as fate would have it, I already had three requests.

The first was a situation like Chloe's, a lady from Texas was having an affair but refused to leave her husband. Not wanting to be the one responsible for the collapse of their marriage, she figured some photos of me with her husband would get her off the hook. It didn't take much considering—I didn't want to do anyone's dirty work anymore. Before I had the chance to decline her offer, she messaged to say her father-in-law had passed away. Her husband was set to inherit a large sum of money, so she'd decided to stay.

Then there was option two, with a twist. It was a husband looking for help this time. He lived in Florida, had been married for six years, and suspected his wife was cheating on him with not one but two women. Having limited experience with lesbianism, I wasn't sure if I'd be the best fit for the job. My cousin, Jet, was a lesbian. She often shared intimate details about her relationships, so I was familiar with her standpoint, but other than that, the only time I had personally experienced a woman's touch in my early twenties.

* * *

Jet had called asking if I wanted to tag along, she was heading to a house party at the "the old frat house," a large converted two-story house close to a hundred and fifty years old. The once-beautiful family home, now run down, was oozing with hormone-filled college students wanting to exert their youthful energies on drinking and sex.

When we arrived, the party had already started, and several kegs blocked the front entrance, waiting their turn to be tapped. Making our way to the side, squeezing through the packed doorway, we were motioned toward the kitchen by some drunk party-goers who showed us the way to the alcohol supply. The kitchen—riddled with beer cups, pizza boxes, and bowls of chips—looked like it had seen better days. A few of the cupboard doors had been ripped off their hinges and the walls displayed several small random holes where pictures should have hung.

A group of frat boys stood around a keg, dispensing the cheap liquid into Solo cups. The plastic holders were on a table nearby. I had three colors to pick from: traditional red, lime green, and hot pink. Picking the pink, my favorite color, I stood in line behind Jet. She had already filled two red cups to the brim before I'd finished deciding on my color. Polishing off her first beer, she started on the second cup while I loaded mine. Jet liked to double fist her drinks; she had a good liver.

The last drop of yellow liquid landed in my cup, and Jet was already off, heading toward a group of young men, waving at them and tipping her cup to her lips, multi-tasking with ease. Before I could follow, the keg's keepers, some jocks who had helped pour my drink, pulled me into conversation. We chatted about their college lives and my job. They were impressed I worked at the Chic Chick . . . according to them, only hot women could get a job there.

While basking in their attention, I felt someone's hip push lightly into mine; it was Jet's roommate, Amber. Happy to see each other, we embraced. She was the type of person everyone loved: joyful, smart, and funny. We'd hit it off from day one, having met the year before when I'd gone to visit Jet at her apartment. Amber and I had several things in common: a passion for life, a love for others, and . . . innovative thinking. We joked often about opening a business together. Often, we sat for hours, putting our creative minds together searching for an ingenious idea. Nothing! Then we'd laugh, concluding perhaps we weren't as creative as we'd once thought!

Beautiful, smart, ambitious, and determined, that was Amber. Her only weakness? *Beautiful* women.

Waving good-bye to the keg boys and preferring to chat with Amber, I'd caught up with her on our lives and we'd even taken a few stabs at some business "ideas" before going to find Jet.

A captive audience had gathered around her. Jet was a natural storyteller and could read a crowd. They were smiling and laughing while she told a tale involving her first boyfriend, a biochemistry class, and the process of photosynthesis. We walked in half way through the story and by the time she'd finished, the group was doubled over in laughter. Not even knowing the humor in the punch line, but getting caught up in the infectious laughter, I laughed too.

Looking around the room, everyone seemed to be enjoying themselves; a cute blonde was laughing uncontrollably at a short, thin male who was on all fours, bucking like a bull. He motioned for her to climb on his back and she did.

Bucking her lightly, she slapped his butt, making him snort louder. Shaking my head, I smiled, taking a sip from my hot pink Solo cup. Empty. Needing a top-up, I made my way back to the keg.

The kitchen had filled with additional scholars, there to kill some of their precious and limited brain cells with alcohol, some sitting on the countertops, some standing, but most, still, around the keg. A jock pushed back the lever to fill the cup, giving me a sexy smile and flexing his muscles. Having mastered his pouring skills, he lifted the lever back just as the beer hit the rim of my cup. I took a moment to admire his forearms peeking out from beneath his fitted shirt.

"So, come here often?" A grin stretched across his face, looking even sexier than I'd first judged.

"Yes . . . when I'm invited. My cousin, Jet." I pointed to her, making faces at the crowd while telling another story. "She's studying economics."

"Never been interested in school?"

"Not really. Working at the Chic Chick pays too well." I laughed. Muscle man knew where I worked, having been one of the boys, around the keg, I'd been speaking with before Amber had arrived.

"A pretty face like yours shouldn't be wasted behind a book anyhow," he counselled, trying to compliment, missing the mark.

Did he think all pretty girls should just carry a tray? I didn't dare ask, for fear I might not like his answer. Enjoying our flirtations, I didn't want to muddle things up. My lack of response was his opening to promote himself, bragging he had single-handedly organized the party. Apparently, he oversaw all the social functions at the old house and wanted to host a Solo-cup-themed party the following week. The purpose? To help people find a mate. The Solo No More Party he wanted to call it; I liked his play on words and laughed.

It gave him fuel to carry on and I listened, nodding my head approvingly. His focus was to set up people at the party by using Solo cups. A red Solo cup meant you were looking for a relationship. A green cup meant you were in a relationship, unavailable but just wanting to hang out. And pink? You were looking for something temporary; a hook up.

"Yeah, so the color of your cup would dictate your availability. Pretty cool, eh?"

I was impressed and amused by his ideas, thinking I'd share them with Amber; perhaps a business idea lurked in the midst? He continued to talk, changing the subject to his last football game, where he'd scored two touchdowns with the help of his teammates.

Attractive, charming, and funny, I thought, waving my pink Solo cup his way, hoping he'd catch my hint. Continuing, I listened, liking his sexy Southern drawl.

As I was considering Mr. Muscles' qualities, I caught a glimpse of Jet and Amber heading up the stairs and excused myself, wanting to pick Amber's brain about an idea: an adult board game using Solo cups. I wasn't exactly sure what the game would entail at this early stage but nonetheless wanted to present the concept to her.

Excusing myself, assuring him I'd return, I neared the stairs. Reaching the top step, I could hear their voices and laughter coming from inside the bedroom door. Turning, I retraced my steps back to the ground floor, knowing better than to interrupt them.

Jet liked to share her sexual experiences with me and I knew she and Amber liked sneaking away halfway through the night to have sex, enjoying the appeal of public places. They'd been living together as college roommates and had come to enjoy having an open relationship.

Jet and Amber appeared in the kitchen holding hands sometime later; it had been wise not to follow. I was in the midst of conversation when Amber swooped in, taking me by the hand, leading me to the dance floor.

The loud music reverberated through ours bodies as we swayed on the makeshift dance floor. The living room table and couches had been pushed to the side, making room for the heap of dancing bodies. The house had no cooling system—the air hot and dense. My hair, moist, clung to my face and sweat ran between my breasts. The wires of my new bra dug into my skin, aching.

Feeling liberal from my intoxication, I removed my bra, placing it on the wall alongside the others—the old frat house rules encouraged such behavior. A display of female delights on the walls and ceiling decorated the house with an array of colors.

The young bodies continued to press into each other, forming one large mass. I closed my eyes—my breasts were enjoying the freedom—letting the movements of the figures surrounding me set the pace, when I suddenly felt it . . . a hand delicately touched my breast and someone's body purposefully and intently pressed into mine.

Turning, hoping to see Mr. Muscles, I was surprised! Staring back at me were Amber's deep brown eyes. I stepped back, thinking she'd mistaken me for someone else, perhaps my cousin? But she smiled coyly. There was no mistake. Her intentions were evident. The lack of space on the dance floor pushed us together again.

I knew Amber was in a relationship with my cousin, but I also knew it was open. Never considering a woman as a partner, still curious, I lingered, letting our bodies move closer. I could feel her breasts on mine as our bodies moved in unison with the crowd. Feeling uneasy, I tipped back the rest of my beer to help me relax, but it didn't help; I started to pull away. Before I could slip from her grasp, a soft hand slid under my top, delicately making its way to my breasts. The approval on her face when she noticed I had no bra was unmistakable—artfully she teased my nipples.

I looked around. No one had taken notice. We were so packed together, and everyone was so drunk, they were oblivious to our indiscretions.

Intrigued, having never been touched by a woman before, I let her continue to touch me, waiting to see if my body would respond. I could tell she was already aroused, her groin pushed into my leg, pulsating as our hot sweaty bodies rubbed against each other. Amber rested her cheek on my shoulder and I could feel the vibrations of her moaning on my skin.

She continued to gently pinch my nipples, her soft touch delicate and skilled, but my body wasn't responding. She looked at me questioningly and motioned toward the stairs, wanting to continue our escapades.

Politely, I declined, shaking my head. "I'm sorry, Amber, but it's just not for me." She didn't appear to be upset; she kissed my neck and withdrew her hands, smiling.

* * *

Jet had been amused when I told her what had happened with Amber. They'd continued their relationship for the next four months until Amber dropped out of college, choosing to open a business instead. Last I'd heard, she'd done very well for herself and was still happily single.

Considering my lack of interest in the same sex I knew I probably wasn't the person for the Florida job either, but before I declined his offer I decided to do a little research and flicked on the television in my hotel room.

The French were known for two things, their beautiful language, and their expertise on sex. Nestling into the oversized gray cuddle chair with its light, furry pink pillows I slipped my legs underneath me. The round chair was large enough to sit two adults, but I enjoyed it solo. I'd finished my cappuccino and made myself some tea. Placing my piping hot cup of peppermint tea on the end table, I picked up the remote, sifting through the ample amount of porn for purchase. There were several options and after ten minutes, I chose a clip of a thin brunette with an ample chest and a bleached blonde who was also well endowed. Watching the video for several minutes, unaroused, I switched the channel.

The screen lit up with a beautiful specimen of a male, perfect in all the right places—my preference confirmed. I wouldn't be able to pull off the Florida gig. His wife would see right through me.

I was going for option number three…

Chapter 28
Annabelle

"MAY I SPEAK WITH BREE PLEASE?"

"Speaking." I answered pleasantly.

"Yes, hello. I emailed you a few days ago but haven't had the chance to call. My apologies for the delay. I got your name from Samantha. She's a dear friend of mine. I live in Wisconsin, in a small town called St. Cloud. My husband is an airline pilot who charters vacationers to Mexico. I suspect his layovers in Mexico are not . . ." She paused. ". . . all business. But I can't prove it. Do you think you can help?"

"Yes. I'm sure of it," I assured her.

"I need complete discretion with this matter. Samantha assured me you can provide this." She continued before I could answer. "Can you start on Friday?"

She was all business, with little emotion. I liked her already. Currently at the airport, soon to be flying back from Europe, I was limited with my conversation, due to the multitude of passengers around me, so I matched her business-like manner, playing it cool. "Yes. Friday works.

Can you send your contact information? I'll call when my flight is booked. What time of day suits you best?"

"Let me check my schedule." Papers rustled in the background before she answered. "Friday my schedule is clear, so any time Friday." She was straight to the point, with no room for small talk.

"OK, I'll aim for Friday afternoon. It's Anabelle, right?" Samantha had called two weeks prior, explaining her friend, Annabelle, would be contacting me. I was pleased with the referral and delighted her friend had finally reached out.

"Yes . . . pardon me! I didn't say who was calling. Annabelle with two n's. My husband's name is Jayson."

"Well Annabelle with two n's, I look forward to meeting you soon." She didn't laugh at my joke; I'd failed to stay professional.

In a tight voice, she replied, "I'll send you additional arrangements after I receive your flight information. You can contact me at the number on your call display now."

"I'll book within the hour," I advised. We said our goodbyes and hung up.

Flipping through my phone, I searched for flights to Wisconsin. Looking at my pink suitcase, I thought, *had I known how much traveling was in store for me after I'd visited Canada, I would have bought two!* I sure missed Chloe, despite what she'd done. I wondered if she knew the domino effect she'd caused in my life. *Regardless,* I thought as I hit the confirm payment option, *things were looking up.*

Chapter 29
St. Cloud, Wisconsin

ANNABELLE PICKED ME UP AT THE AIRPORT ON Friday, the day she'd requested I arrive, and we drove to St. Cloud in silence. As expected from our previous conversation, she wasn't much for small talk. Thirty minutes later, we arrived; it was welcoming and quiet. Trying to break the ice, I asked a few questions about St. Cloud. She explained it was one of many bedroom communities surrounding the city of Milwaukee, with a population of nearly 20,000 people. The suburb was big enough to have most of the necessary amenities but without the overcrowded population of the city.

The community was very clean and appeared to be inhabited by wealthy people. The townsfolk were extremely friendly—several people waved as we passed—and life seemed pleasant in St. Cloud, as the name might suggest. Well-kept wives with no more than two children frequented the streets, ushering their children here and there.

Surprisingly, Annabelle continued to talk. I'd found her weak spot. She was obviously very fond of her home town. Annabelle explained many families chose to live in St. Cloud to be away from city life as it provided their children with a better upbringing. According to her, most of the wives she knew stayed at home because their husbands had well-paying jobs in the city and worked long hours. Her only complaint—cheating was not uncommon in their community, with a number of marriage failures per year as a result.

It was easy to see Annabelle was a loyal, loving soul. Despite her tough exterior, she was genuine, with a big heart. Starting to feel at ease, she began talking about her children, her face lighting up as she did. It was apparent she was very proud of them. She loved caring for them and filled her days with playing, cooking and baking, and she even cleaned her own home. Normally the wives of St. Cloud had maids, but she'd never bothered, taking pride in doing it herself. Although life in St. Cloud was enjoyable, it lacked depth, she said.

Her eyes sad, she focused on the road, deep in thought. "I could do like some of the others—enjoy the money and turn a blind eye…not what I want for my children or myself. Sure, it's nice to have beautiful things and to stay at home with the kids, but what good is all this without a faithful husband. Our life is a lie. I'm in love with my husband and want to believe his constant assurances he's not cheating, but I feel in my heart he's lying."

"What makes you think he's cheating?" I ventured to ask.

"I have several examples. I'll give you the latest one. He was in Mexico on a layover last night. I called his room every hour last night and he never answered the phone. He's returning home today, at around midnight, and his excuse will be 'You must have called the wrong room, Babe'," she sighed, "By the way, he's used that line before."

Memories of Adam came rushing back. I'd done the same thing, calling his hotel room to check up on him, using the same tactic to catch him cheating. Feeling a pang in my heart, I too looked straight ahead with burdened eyes.

She didn't shed any tears. No, by this time she'd become numb, most likely emotionally checked out—the constant pain from her husband's perceived betrayals turning her into a zombie.

"Sometimes, I think I'm going crazy," she confessed as she waved to another young mother with a newborn in her arms. "He says all the right things. His excuses end up seeming legit, making me out to be the paranoid one, so I eventually cave, feeling guilty for even suspecting him."

Trying to be helpful, I offer some information. "I've heard its common for men who cheat to make their partner feel guilty. It's a reverse psychology thing."

She shook her head in agreement. "I've heard the same and it's not just the excuses I find troubling but his lack of physical interest in me as well. On several occasions he's been too tired to be intimate."

In her late thirties, tall, thin, beautiful, and elegant, I couldn't imagine Jayson not being attracted to her. Negatively, I thought, *he's probably getting it someplace else!* I didn't dare acknowledge her suspicions until we had the truth and it was time to face them.

"Then there's the late-night calls. I can hear a female voice on the other end, but he insists its work; he doesn't work with any female co-pilots."

She was looking straight ahead, still in a daze. She was not only beautiful, like the other wives of St. Cloud we'd passed along the streets, but she also had an inner beauty. I envied her, being so dedicated to her husband despite her suspicions. I could see she longed for a normal and healthy family life but was fading away emotionally from the toxicity her husband had injected into their lives. She didn't fit into St. Cloud's soap-opera life. The drama didn't suit her.

"We'll get to the bottom of this, once and for all," I promised.

My assertive tone shook her out of her dreary thoughts and she turned to me and offered a weak smile. "I sure hope so. I sure hope so." She reached over, squeezed my shoulder and nodded.

Had I managed to give hope to a tiny piece of her hardened heart?

Their home, traditional yet stunning, was huge, and gauging from the massive exterior, probably 6,000 square feet. The foyer, about the size of my condo, was elegantly finished. Annabelle's home was warm, a contemporary country look with a touch of flair. Despite its grandeur it felt cozy.

"Wow, beautiful!" I exclaimed, setting my suitcase down.

"Well, thanks," she blushed. The pitter patter of little feet came toward us. "I told the kids you were the new decorator. Please play along." I nodded as they barreled toward her, squealing in delight, chanting, "Mommy! Mommy! Mommy!"

The three bundles of energy came running into her loving arms, all looking to be under the age of nine, and fit perfectly into her embrace. She squeezed them tightly and they squirmed under her kisses. Standing up, she introduced me to her trio of joy. "Children, this is Bree. Our new decorator."

"Hello, Bree," they all chimed in unison with bright eyes and rosy cheeks.

"Well, hello darlings." With the biggest smile I could manage, I knelt beside them, so I could tickle their little bellies and pinch their chubby dimpled cheeks. They giggled and squirmed, liking the attention.

"Enough children," a voice barked, scolding them. On command, they instantly stopped, motionless. Looking up, I saw a lady standing behind them. Distracted by the children I hadn't seen her enter the room. She continued with her commands. "Run along children. I'll be up in the toy room shortly to finish the puzzle with you. I need a minute to speak with the *decorator*."

She was an older perfect likeness to Annabelle in both attitude and appearance. The little ones took off running and giggling, waving good-bye as they rounded the corner. "This must be your mom," I guessed, extending my hand to the older attractive lady. "My name is Bree. Pleased to meet you."

Her back was perfectly straight as she reached for my hand, shaking it firmly then pressing her hands neatly together. "As I am you. We are so very happy to have you here. Annabelle has explained how you can assist. She's been troubled for many years with this ailment in her life. I'm glad she's finally doing something about it." Annabelle's mother commanded respect and exuded confidence. She was the kind of woman who made things happen and was looking forward to a resolution for her daughter's sake. "I'll be in the toy room if needed, but I assume you can handle this on your own, Annabelle."

She didn't wait for Annabelle's response. She just nodded and turned around. We watched in silence as she walked away. Her mother was dressed for a day at the country club, not a day in the toy room, but from what I had gathered during my short interactions with her, she would not be seen in anything else. She looked like a resident of St. Cloud: rich, beautiful, and well-groomed.

"She's a strong woman, your mom." Our eyes followed her as she exited the room.

"Indeed, she is. That's what spurred my calling you. My mother knows I suspect Jayson, and I told her what you did for Samantha; she respects Samantha's opinion but wanted to meet you first, so she suggested I bring you to the house before proceeding. You have her approval; if you didn't, she would have said otherwise. As you can see, she doesn't mince words."

I could hear the kids laughing in the background and wondered how her husband could take advantage of one of life's greatest treasures, a family who loved him.

"Samantha didn't go into detail about what happened between you and Evan, but she explained the procedure and assured me you would find a solution to my problem. So here we are." Reaching into her purse, she pulled out an envelope. "Here's the plane ticket."

She'd sent two emails the day before my arrival. The first one being a money transfer of $30,000, my agreed-upon fee, and the second informing she would be purchasing an airline ticket on my behalf. The ticket was for the next flight her husband was piloting to Mexico, which was on Sunday, in two days' time.

She ran her fingers along the edges and over the top, delaying the transaction. I knew she wanted answers but would be saddened by the truth if her suspicions were validated.

"Are you sure you want to do this?" I asked.

She was speechless for several minutes before continuing. "I have nothing left inside. My marriage has been a death by a thousand cuts, so many small hurts over a long period of time has left me void of emotion. It wasn't always like this, we loved each other very deeply, but that was long ago. Although, I am forever hopeful you come back empty-handed, and perhaps the wounds can heal eventually, and we can be happy again. Maybe you can save my marriage. I need this. I need to know. I need answers."

With the back of her hand, she wiped a tear from her cheek. It was the first time I'd seen her lose composure. Handing the envelope over, she asserted, "Yes, I'm ready."

I took it gingerly from her delicate hands and slipped it into my purse, wanting to hide the offensive envelope from her view. Swallowing hard, readying myself to ask a difficult question, I probed, "Annabelle, I know this may be difficult, but I need to know what your husband likes, doesn't like."

She raised an eyebrow, not sure where I was going.

Hesitantly, but this time more clearly, I asked, "What's the best way to tempt your husband? Do you have any suggestions?"

Her face dropped, and through pursed lips she said in a measured voice, "I'm sorry but I have no suggestions and you shouldn't need my help. It gives you an unfair advantage."

Gracefully, she smoothed out her clothing, preparing herself to leave, and motioned towards the front door.

"I need to see my kids. I'll call you a cab and you can see yourself out. I'll expect to hear from you when your job is complete. Thank you for your time. I apologize for my abruptness, but this isn't easy for me."

Without looking back, she headed in the same direction her children and mother had taken. I made my way out and shortly after into a cab.

Heading to my hotel, taking in the streets of St. Cloud from the backseat, I felt even more determined to help Annabelle find answers and dared to hope she was wrong. Maybe I could help mend their marriage. I contemplated what Annabelle had said; she was right, it would give me an unfair advantage. If Jayson were going to cheat, he was going to cheat. This wasn't the same situation as Evan. Samantha knew positively Evan was cheating. Evan had been paying high-class hookers for their silence, so I had needed the extra bait to help catch him.

This time I was going in blind, naïve to Jayson's psyche...

Chapter 30
Jayson and the wolf pack

SITTING AT GATE FIFTEEN, WAITING TO BOARD, I smoothed out my dress and played with my hair, impatiently waiting to head south with many other guests. Annabelle had instructed me on Jayson's pre-flight rituals, so I was expecting him to pass by the front counter at any time.

Waiting for him, I admired my freshly lacquered nails. Annabelle had lodged me at a spa hotel in the city, paying for everything in full. The salon had done an excellent job of my pedicure, manicure, coloring, and waxing. Every inch of my body had been pampered. My hair, now back to its normal light golden brown, was styled straight, looking very silky.

The only spa experience I hadn't enjoyed was the waxing. A middle-aged lady with jet black hair, my torturer, was proficient but ruthless at her job, and I winced in pain under her efforts. As she was removing the third strip from in between my legs, I recalled the countless visits to the salon I had taken before meeting up with Adam. I'd gone for the exact same procedure when I was his full-time mistress. I didn't miss the time spent perfecting every inch of my body, so it would be in prime shape, ready on demand like a take-out dinner. I preferred being a mistress for hire. At least then there was a purpose behind the primping and priming.

My rose-colored nail polish complimented my tan. I'd spent several hours sandwiched inside a tanning booth, located beside the hotel's indoor pool, in a skimpy bikini to ensure minimal tan lines. My browned skin accentuated my toned arms, which I'd given a few extra hours at the gym the day before. I enjoyed working out. The feeling of my muscles responding to physical activity always gave me a natural high. The two days at the hotel had given me the occasion to perfect my look and it was time to put my efforts to use. I was ready.

For my flight to Mexico, I'd decided to slip on a cream fitted dress with nothing underneath. I wanted to make sure Jayson noticed me straight away and hoped the lack of undergarment outlines would only assist in my endeavors. It was clear I had gone commando. This was something Chloe would have done, and I was taking a page from her book today. My outfit, fitting my curves to precision and hugging all the right places, was perfect for the occasion.

According to Annabelle, he boarded the plane roughly forty-five minutes before take-off, and at exactly forty-seven minutes, there he was, walking toward the gate, flanked by two pretty flight attendants who were gushing over him. He was grinning ear to ear, enjoying their attention, pulling his suitcase with one hand, and placing his other free hand on the lower back of one of the stewardesses.

He was already looking like a player, but I tried to refrain from making a judgment until we spoke. Jayson was cute enough—rich black hair with not an ounce of gray, which was surprising for his age. Annabelle had told me he was forty-six, older than his wife. She'd married him because he'd proven to be mature and family-oriented, presumably. He carried a few extra pounds around his middle, but it was acceptable for a man his age, and from my point of view, a few feet away, he looked to be about six feet tall. For the most part, he'd kept his looks and was in relatively good shape. He was confident and evidently well-liked by the ladies. I rated him at 6.5 out of 10, allotting an extra half mark for the uniform because I liked men in uniforms.

They approached the check-in area before accessing the plane and were greeted by two additional attractive ladies, who also vied for his attention. Mr. Popular had a harem of ladies at his disposal.

Sitting in the front row near the check-in area, I was impatiently waiting for him to take notice, but he was surrounded by so many distractions he hadn't even looked around. After watching him flirt shamelessly with the staff, I grew impatient as I thought of his three young children waiting for him at home and became even more determined.

I got up and headed over to the front counter, making sure to announce my arrival by placing myself in his line of direct sight. It didn't take him long to notice. The full effect of my fitted dress burned itself into his pupils. His mouth dropped and his eyes widened in approval. All four women surrounding him turned to follow his gaze and their smiles dissolved. Exactly the introduction I was hoping for! I had everyone's attention, including the harem.

My boarding pass safely tucked away in my purse, I asked, "Excuse me, but I seem to have misplaced my boarding pass. Could I please have another re-issued?" I smiled sweetly and politely, hoping he'd answer first.

'His ladies' could see through my charms, and the least pretty of the four hissed at me, "You'll have to wait until everyone is boarded and then we can assist you. Please take your seat back in the waiting area." She pointed in the direction of my seat, hoping I would obey like a disciplined puppy. I didn't budge, instead looking over at Jayson with large doe eyes, pleading for his help.

He took the carrot. "Now, Beth," Jayson beamed at me, not even looking her way. I could feel his eyes taking in every inch of my body. "Let's help this pretty young lady get a new pass."

"Of course, captain." Beth nodded, changing her tune after Jayson came to my defence.

He clearly ran the show and his 'wolf pack' jumped when he barked. I couldn't help but stifle a little laugh at their mindless obedience. Luckily, my humor at their expense went unnoticed.

"Better yet, let's give her an upgrade to first class."

His eyes were still taking me in. Beth started to lose her patience, despite her original obedience. Her captain was fussing over someone outside the pack and it was unacceptable.

Through tight lips, she murmured, "We don't have any first-class seats left."

"Really? The girls just told me on the way over first class was only at 70 percent capacity. So, let's help Miss . . . What's your name, beautiful?"

"Bree," I smiled and giggled, mimicking one of his pack members, knowing from my brief observations he liked women who gushed over him—I followed suit.

"I'll see what I can do, captain." Beth smiled forcefully my way, then sweetly at him.

Placing his hand on my elbow, he veered me away from the front desk, looking for privacy. Once we were a couple of feet away, I continued to gush over him. "Thank you so much." I placed my hand on his chest. "How can I ever repay you? I've had such a bad month; it's nice to be spoiled."

"And why is that?" He moved his hand to the small of my back, obviously a spot his hand liked to inhabit when he spoke with the opposite sex.

"My boyfriend dumped me, so I'm headed to Mexico to help erase his memory. My girlfriend, who lives a couple of states away, is coming to help re-introduce me to the *single* life again." I batted my eyelashes, inviting him to join the festivities. My new lash extensions were full and long, framing my light blue eyes, making them look large and innocent.

"I could gaze at those blue eyes all day," he complimented in a sultry voice. He had no shame, and from what I could tell, he was probably sleeping with at least one of the flight attendants, likely Beth, yet he flirted openly without concern. "Why don't you come visit me in the *cockpit* to discuss repayment?" He massaged the small of my back.

"You've made my day. I'll do *anything* to repay you." I flirted back, equally unabashed.

Beth loudly announced the pre-boarding call and motioned Jayson over to her booth. "I'll see you soon." He ran his hand over my bottom and gave it a light tap.

As he approached his girls, they surrounded him like a pack protecting its young, happy he was within their grasp yet again. They fussed over him for several minutes before I saw him whispering something into Beth's ear. Jayson motioned me toward the front counter, securing my spot in first class, then advanced down the ramp.

I thought to myself, *Bree: one, wolf pack: zero.*

I had taken the lead . . .

Chapter 31
Code name: Maverick

BETH TOOK UP A POSITION BEHIND THE COMPUTER and pressed down heavily on the keyboard, taking out her frustrations. After an extra-long inspection of my passport, hoping to find a flaw in my documentation, wanting to deny me access to her precious captain, she gave up and let me board.

The poor service continued. At the mouth of the plane, I was greeted by the two pretty flight attendants who had accompanied Jayson on his walk to the front counter. Unfortunately, they were looking after first class.

"Welcome aboard," they growled simultaneously through clenched teeth, smiles forced. They ushered me forward, neglecting their duties, not locating my seat. Advancing into the aisleway, I eventually spotted my seat four rows down. Beth had conveniently assigned me the seat closest to the washroom, implementing her revenge.

Making my way down the aisle, I was starting to wonder if all the staff were crazy, when I caught a glimpse of the co-pilot standing in line, waiting to use the restroom. An elderly lady with jet blue hair arrived behind him and started to shift uncomfortably. He offered his spot in line, which she took greedily and without thanks. When I arrived at my seat, the co-pilot was still waiting for the elderly lady to exit.

"It was thoughtful of you to offer your place in line," I narrowed my eyes, reading his name tag, "Maverick,"

"Thanks for noticing." He said, looking very fetching in his uniform.

"I sure did, and this might seem a little forward, but is that your real name or did you perhaps borrow it from the movie?"

He put his hands in the air. "You caught me. I stole it from the movie. It's my wing name, the one I use when I'm piloting this bird." He tapped the wall of the plane, taking ownership. "My real name is Madoc."

"Maverick, Madoc, the names are very similar. I can see why you picked it."

I could be myself now: no flirting, no teasing, no acting, just friendly banter.

The elderly lady suddenly and forcefully opened the bathroom door, hitting Madoc in the back. Stepping forward to keep his balance, his foot nearly landed on mine.

"I'm so sorry. Are you OK?" He backed away, concerned. The little old lady with the blue hair was already halfway down the aisle, unaware she'd just smacked the co-pilot in the back.

"I'm fine. My toes are intact." I teased.

"Whew! Thank goodness. Wow, that's one strong grandma! I'm going to get a membership to whatever gym she goes to," he joked, rubbing his back.

As we talked about the lady with the lovely blue hair, I took him in. He looked maybe a year or two older than me. His hair was light brown and his eyes a light gray. His features were strong and manly: a square jaw and chiseled cheek bones. His uniform outlined his lean, muscular body. He was at least 6'3", which I liked because it complimented my 5'7" frame. He had no ring; I had made sure to look. Therefore, he was probably single, ruggedly handsome, and had a good job. He'd have been a nice catch to bring home to my parents, but I wasn't here for my own personal agenda.

I could hear a sigh in the distance and felt eyes burning a hole through the back of my head. It had to be one of the flight attendants—not happy I was talking to another one of *her* pilots. My analysis was correct.

"Please take your seat, ma'am. You're blocking the aisle." She scowled.

Madoc and I looked around the aisle and then at each other, shrugging at the same time; there was no one, but we weren't prepared to take on an ill-tempered flight attendant. I took my seat, not wanting to provoke her any longer. Madoc disappeared into the washroom and resurfaced a few minutes later. Leaning over, he whispered, "It was nice meeting you. I hope you have a wonderful time in Mexico!"

"I enjoyed meeting you too. Thank you, Maverick." I flicked his name tag and winked.

Madoc walked to the front of the plane and tried to enter the flight deck but was blocked by members of Jayson's pack. He didn't appear anywhere near as comfortable with their advances as Jayson. Instead, he created as much distance as possible, but with the plane's limited space it was difficult, and their tentacles were far-reaching. Every time one of them would touch his arm, he would lean in the opposite direction.

After fighting off their advances for several minutes, he was saved by an announcement asking everyone to be seated for the safety demonstration. Madoc escaped into the flight deck and the two flight attendants positioned themselves, ready to demonstrate the safety procedures. As they stood in the middle of the aisle, looking poised and professional pointing to the emergency exits, one of the flight attendants glared in my direction with complete disdain—I figured it was best not to order any food or beverages unless they were in a sealed container, just to be on the safe side.

A short time later, we took flight, and I flipped open my laptop. I'd downloaded several movies and I was half way through the first one when I felt a tap on my shoulder. It was a new face, a friendlier one. "Hello, miss. The captain was wondering if you wanted to see the flight deck."

I looked around for Jayson's guard dogs, worried they might attack, but they were nowhere to be found. A change in staff had most likely been effected by Jayson to protect me. "That would be lovely. Thank you."

"Please follow me," she said, gesturing toward the front of the plane. I got up, positioning myself behind her.

On the walk over, I realized there was another fresh face taking care of first class, a promising sign I was making headway if Jayson had gone through so much trouble to see me.

Outside the door of the flight deck, she closed the curtains tight, hiding us from any curious passengers, and called into the cabin using a phone by the door. I overheard a male voice asking for a password, which she provided.

The door clicked open, she ushered me inside, and quickly closed the door. I knew I wasn't supposed to be on deck, but Jayson was senior in service and apparently had a lot of pull.

With the door closed immediately at my back, my chest constricted and anxiety started to build. I didn't care for small spaces. I took in the massive display of the ultra-modern gadgets. The front of the plane was cluttered with electronical and technical instruments, which overwhelmed most of the area. There were two pilot seats, occupied by Jayson and Madoc. They looked at ease and pleased to see me. Madoc was first to speak. "Hello, sunshine." His smile was genuine, showing off his polished teeth. His authenticity instantly relaxed my chest muscles—the release like taking off a pair of tight shoes after a long walk.

Taking in a large breath, I exclaimed, "This is amazing. How do you manage all this?"

No acting required. I was impressed. Madoc started to explain the Coles notes version of flying when Jayson rudely interrupted, leaned back in his throne, and declared, "Madoc's only the co-pilot, honey . . . this is my bird." His upper body protruded with pride. He looked like an ape about to beat his chest! "Besides this is a little too technical for a pretty gal like you." He winked and tapped my rear. I giggled, pretending to slap his hand away in a weak protest.

I glanced over at Madoc, who looked perplexed and disappointed. *Was he crushing on me too?* Having the choice, my attention would be his, but I was there for Jayson.

Jayson caught me looking at Madoc a little too long, and now it was his turn to be jealous. I inwardly cursed myself for being so easily distracted and refocused my attention.

Leaning in, making sure my breasts were pressed into his arm, resting on the captain's chair, I whispered into his ear, "Baby, I'm going to rip that uniform off your body as soon as I get you alone."

I was working on instinct, knowing his type, and by the looks of Jayson's glowing green eyes, I was spot-on.

Jayson eagerly reached into his right pocket, pulling out his business card. Flipping it over, he instructed Madoc to lend him a pen. Madoc tossed one over, unhappy with its intended use. As Jayson was jotting down his personal cell number, I couldn't help but look over at Madoc again. He looked at me with big eyes and angled his gaze toward the captain's chair, mouthing the words, "*Be careful.*"

His concern for my well-being despite my shameful actions surprised me. I quickly looked away, ill-at-ease, not wanting Jayson to catch me again. He put the pen in his shirt pocket and handed me his card. As I took it, he boldly kissed the top of my hand. "I'm looking forward to seeing you soon."

Once back in my seat, I could feel a headache coming on, the stress of becoming someone's mistress was draining. It seemed headaches were becoming a norm since starting my new career! Rummaging through my purse, looking for some Advil, I came up empty-handed. I lay my head back and closed my eyes, hoping sleep would help.

Chapter 32
Mr. Sandman

THE AXE BLADE GLIMMERED IN THE SUN. SHE RAISED the cutting tool above her head, looking down and glaring at a newborn kitten laying on the grass. The kitten's eyes were still firmly shut, not having had the chance to open yet, still wet from its mother's womb. And although the kitten couldn't see the enemy above, it sensed its presence, already knowing evil in its first moments of life.

The kitten struggled to stand, trying to find balance, only to collapse, meowing desperately looking for its mother's protection.

In a moment of pity, the girl laid down the axe, blood dripping from the blade, suddenly reconsidering the newborn kitten's fate. Caressing the scratch inflicted upon her by the kitten's mother while protecting her young, the butcher contemplated her next move.

"Maybe you'll be nicer than your mother. Maybe you deserve a chance. Your mommy had a little accident, she won't be around anymore, but I'll keep you *if* you're good."

She hovered over the helpless kitten, still trying to decide its fate. The kitten cried out and helplessly swiped the air. "Oh, kitty, look what you've done now. You're acting just like your mama. I don't like being upset because I do *silly* things when I'm upset," she bemoaned then laughed to herself. "Bad little kitty," she purred in a soft voice. "I won't hurt you."

She picked up the hysteric kitten in her palms and began to stroke it softly and calmly. After several minutes, the loud cries turned into soft whimpers, which turned into the kitten's first purr as trust and comfort were established inside the girl's soothing hands.

Snap!

Silence.

The executioner removed her fingers from around the kitten's neck, the wet bundle of fur now lifeless in her hands. She continued to stroke it while singing to the tune of a popular lullaby, "Hush little kitty, don't you purr 'cause your mama's dead and there's no cure."

Humored by her impromptu song, she laughed uncontrollably while repeating the verse louder and louder, skipping toward a nearby pig pen; tossing the carcass inside.

This time, she thought, *no one can ask me about the dead kittens lying around the yard.* Several pigs circled and sniffed before attacking, fighting over the fresh meat. Already finished devouring the mother, they were hungry for seconds. They squealed in delight, as if thanking the culprit for another tasty snack.

Grabbing the axe, wiping off the blood on the tall blades of grass near the pen, she rested it on her shoulder, skipping away, singing her new lullaby, "Hush little kitty. . ." as three large pigs pulled at the kitten's corpse, bones grinding in their teeth . . .

* * *

"Bree! Wake up!"

I jumped.

Madoc was shaking me awake. "Are you OK?"

Wiping the fog from my eyes, I recognized the same look of concern I'd seen on his face in the flight deck. Dazed, I answered, "I just had the *worst* nightmare and you happened to catch me at the end of it!"

"Sorry, I didn't mean to startle you. You were panicked and mumbling; I decided to butt in and help out."

Again, I was flattered by his concern. "Thanks, Madoc." I got up to ease the conversation. "I'm happy you woke me."

"Glad to be of assistance, ma'am." He tipped his pilot hat forward. "Luckily, I happened to be in the area, using the facility." He motioned towards the bathroom door then his eyes darted around the cabin, as if searching for someone. "I was looking for the lovely lady with the blue hair, making sure the coast was clear and I noticed you in distress."

He looked at me fondly and I welcomed the distraction. The memory of the nightmare was still fresh; I shuddered at the thought. Suddenly becoming serious, he loosened his collar and cleared his throat. "I know this is none of my business, but you seem like a really nice gal. I don't think it's a good idea for you to get mixed up with Jayson."

I tried to remain unaffected. "Really and why do you say that?"

"Just trust me. Please stay away."

He baffled me. *Why was this stranger trying to help me, and why was he so concerned about my welfare?* "You sure don't make a good wing man, no pun intended." I laughed. "Aren't you supposed to be helping him out with respect to the ladies?"

"I have a sister, Hannah, and would never want her getting mixed up with a guy like Jayson. She's caring, just like you."

"You don't know anything about me and seem to be making a lot of assumptions." I shook my head, puzzled.

"I disagree. I saw you at the spa hotel in Milwaukee. I was at the same hotel for some meetings, and noticed you on two separate occasions."

"You were spying on me?" I inquired, raising my eyebrows, wondering where this could be going.

"No, not at all. Please don't assume that! It's just . . . you're too beautiful not to notice."

My cheeks went warm from his compliment. I was relieved the plane was dimly lit.

"On both occasions, you were attentive to complete strangers. The first time was by the hotel pool. A mother had come to swim with her twin toddlers, who were about two years old. She was having trouble managing both. You took notice, jumped in, and stayed with them."

He was right. I'd been at the hotel pool, perfecting my tan for Jayson, when I'd noticed a young mother in the pool needing help. The twins had reminded me of Chloe's niece and nephew. We held onto the little ones as they bobbed in and out of the water like baby seals for over an hour. I remembered the experience had left me aching to reach out to Chloe. I missed her and desperately wanted things to be the same between us. I was starting to realize after becoming a mistress for hire that marriage was more complicated than I thought! My initial distain for my oldest and dearest friend was starting to fade. It had all worked out anyhow, hadn't it? Chloe, Brody, and even myself had moved onto greener pastures. I thought to myself, *maybe I should call her? Maybe someday.*

"I didn't even see you!"

"I'm not as easy on the eyes as you, but don't worry, I'm not offended." He winked, and I smiled at his modesty.

"You're extremely handsome. I'm not sure how you went unnoticed," I protested, becoming a little too friendly. I just couldn't help myself.

"Well, it's very flattering of you to say so."

He ran his hands through his thick locks—how I wished I could touch them! We stared at each other, not knowing what to say.

I spoke, wanting to break the silence. "And the second time?" I said, leaning in a little more than needed, taking in the scent of his musky cologne, thinking I smelled a hint of cinnamon too.

"The second time, you were at the hotel restaurant, sitting on the patio, and a gangly fellow approached you. I can only assume he was hitting on you, but you chased him away. He came back a second time and you chased him off again. You got up to leave, most likely to avoid a third attack!"

Madoc chuckled and then carried on. "On your way out, you passed a man in a wheelchair who was on his own, sitting at the bar. He looked to be in a sullen mood. I saw you walk over, order two drinks, and sit down with him. A few minutes later, the pair of you were laughing and telling stories like old friends." Madoc was beaming with admiration. "So you see, my dear, I do know you, and what I witnessed earlier is not the same person from the hotel. What's up?"

The gentleman in the wheelchair had caught my attention that day because he was alone and appeared to be upset. Figuring he needed company and I had time on my hands, I'd gone over to introduce myself. His name was Joe, a war veteran. Not only had he fractured his spine in battle and lost his ability to walk, but his wife had recently been diagnosed with cancer; he was down, but not out. Although plagued with negatives and saddened by them, he kept an optimistic attitude. We talked for hours before parting ways. It turned out he had given more than I, reaffirming my faith in gratitude.

I was surprised Madoc had taken notice of my interactions and was intrigued by his interest. I wanted to share the purpose of my trip with Madoc, but I barely knew him, let alone trusted him. Diverting his attention, not wanting him to pry any longer, I changed the focus. "I think you missed your calling, wingman, perhaps you should have been a detective. How long have you been a pilot, anyhow?"

"Ten years, and I can see you are looking to change the subject, so I will oblige." And he did— "This may sound bold of me, but I like you."

The plane hit turbulence and the seatbelt sign came on. A familiar voice hissed, "Sir, Jayson wants you back in the co-pilot seat. Now!"

It was one of my old friends back in action; the wolf pack had managed to return. Her red nails gripped Madoc's arm, guiding him away from her competition. He challenged and lightly pulled away, but her grip was firm.

Hurriedly, he probed, "Where are you staying?"

She sent a sour face my way, daring me to answer. "At the Plaza Bello," I called after him.

"What are the chances! So am I!" he exclaimed. "I'll see you back at the hotel, then!"

I nodded in agreement while the pretty stewardess grunted at him to hurry up, dragging him back to the flight deck like an undisciplined child.

Madoc was surprised at the coincidence, although I wasn't. Annabelle had made sure to book the same hotel as her husband, so it would make sense Madoc would also be there. Usually the pilots only stayed two nights, but this time, Jayson's layover was longer. The airline company was hosting a four-day conference.

Annabelle had picked this opportunity, hoping four days would be enough. It was already looking like Jayson would be a quick job, so I dared to dream, thinking perhaps after I'd finished with Jayson, I could make some time for Madoc.

Thoughts rolled around inside my head—*what would he think when he found out what I did for a living? Would he be disgusted, intrigued, or both?*

My headache started to return just thinking about it. I needed something to take the edge off. I waited until the fasten seatbelts light went out, then walked to the back of the plane to find a friendlier stewardess. I ordered a glass of wine, to sip slowly while I finished watching my movie. Thankfully, I didn't see Jayson or Madoc again for the rest of the flight.

The plane arrived in Mexico two hours later. I boarded the hotel shuttle. Still no Jayson and Madoc. They would be taking another shuttle, something more private for staff. Annabelle had mentioned this practice. My headache was still pounding. The shuttle was quick, and I checked into the hotel twenty minutes later.

The king-sized bed looked welcoming with its clean white sheets and I fell into it, leaving my trusty pink suitcase unpacked. I planned a short nap before attempting anything else.

Clearing my headache was the first step. After that, I would continue my quest. As I drifted off, I started to plan the best way to insert myself into Jayson's evening. *What was I going to wear?*

Chapter 33
Tick Tock

I WOKE UP WITH A START TO FIND IT WAS 4:10 A.M. I'd managed to sleep my opportunity away. Annabelle was going to be upset. I had limited time to snare him and the conference went all day, leaving evenings only at my disposal.

I checked my phone—no messages. I wasn't off to a good start, however, luckily, Annabelle was giving me some space to do my thing. Laying back on the pillow, I figured there was no sense trying to find Jayson now. He'd be sleeping. I usually didn't oversleep and suspected it was the aftermath of the headache. At least it was gone, and I hadn't dreamed of the psychopath with the axe. I'd never experienced a nightmare quite like it! Loving animals, I was shocked by the brutality. I chalked it up to stress; I had a lot going on.

I was well rested and pumped to go. Hopping out of bed, I started to plan my day. The first choice: which sexy bikini to wear. Having bought several tempting options, I decided on the yellow string bikini with minimal support.

My beach wear was skimpy, not normally items I chose, but I had a purpose.

By 6 a.m. I was poolside, wanting to beat the eager vacationers to a prime spot. I knew Jayson wouldn't be enjoying the amenities until later that day, but I was hoping he'd catch a glimpse of me during his lunch break.

My morning was relaxing, keeping up with my tan as I waited for noon. I could tell it was almost lunch as the hotel guests were making their way over to the buffet. It was time to add a fresh coat of tanning oil; Jayson would be arriving shortly. I wanted to tattoo the image of my scantily clad body on his brain. My intent was to continue to capture Jayson's attention; letting him chase—the reward was sweeter.

Just as I was applying the last of the oil to my legs, he appeared, surrounded by his harem. This time he noticed me right away and grinned possessively in my direction. He anxiously waved me over. I added an extra bounce to my step; making sure my breasts followed the movement. I enjoyed watching his admirers slink off in defeat.

They had all disappeared by the time I arrived. Jayson advanced, placing his hand on the small of my back, true to his favorite move, and pulled me closer.

"Wow! You are stunning! I didn't realize we were at the same hotel until Madoc mentioned it. I was hoping to run into you. Why didn't you call?" He shook his finger disapprovingly. "I'm waiting for you to make good on your promise."

"And what promise is that?" I said, biting my lower lip, playing coy.

"Something about a reward for a seat in first class, if I recall." His hand settled on my rear and he squeezed.

Jayson's hand hadn't been on my bottom for more than a second when Madoc appeared out of nowhere, looking unimpressed. "Hello, Bree," he said, his voice measured. Eyeballing the placement of Jayson's hand, he wasn't taking notice of my bikini at all.

Jayson positioned himself between Madoc and me, as if defending his next meal. "Hey Maverick, why don't you get us a table? The place is filling up fast." Madoc looked at me, hoping for an indication I wanted his help, but I looked away.

"Sure, Jayson. I'll get right on it," he said sarcastically, turning his back on the spectacle, not wishing to be a witness any longer. Madoc stormed away, looking rattled. I was disappointed he'd given up so easily, but then he turned around, announcing loudly across the room, "By the way, Bree, he's *married* with *three* kids. Maybe think on it."

Several hotel guests looked our way and began to whisper. Jayson's smugness turned to damage control, annoyed his wing man had outed him. He quickly recovered. "He's joking. I've been separated for over two years now. He's trying to scare you off because he wants you to himself. I can't blame him."

Jayson's eyes fixated on my sparsely covered breasts. Watching Madoc reluctantly slink off, I started to lose my luster, no longer wanting to play this game. Inwardly, I sighed, refocusing. Leaning in, I whispered, "You can have me tonight baby . . . all night . . . all of me."

His breath deepened, and he panted in approval, pulling my body into his. "Baby, I want you right now!"

Bringing the tip of my finger to my lips and sucking on the tip, I nodded in agreement.

"Call me tonight. Promise?" he pleaded, his eyes wide with excitement.

"Without a doubt," I said, my tone playful. I lightly kissed his cheek before sauntering back to my chaise lounge. I applied another layer of oil while he gawked over his half-eaten hamburger and untouched fries.

After Jayson and his clan had finished lunch, I made my way back to my room. Having accomplished my desired outcome for the morning, it was time to report to my employer. I dialed her number and felt my belly flip, then flop. I disliked the awkward situation of having to tell her about her husband's infidelity. Jayson was proving to be just as easy as Evan.

"Hello, Sadie speaking," said a sweet chanting voice. It dawned on me then: it was Annabelle's daughter Sadie I had dreamed of…she was the girl in my nightmare! But she was *no* cat killer, this was certain. Somehow, I'd twisted the image of this sweet child into some weird nightmare.

The hairs on the back of my neck stood at attention. I could sense danger. *The dream was warning me of something, but what?* I was still trying to decipher the meaning of my nightmare when Annabelle came to the line. "Hello?"

"Hi Annabelle! It's me, Bree."

"Yes, I know who it is. Why are you calling? I sent you a message not to call. I want internet-based messages only.

Jayson called last night asking who I knew in New York. He's checking the phone logs."

She was straight to the point as always. I paused, feeling embarrassed at having called.

"I haven't given my number to Jayson nor do I plan to. He won't know you called me."

"You've talked to him already?" The disbelief in her voice was evident.

"Yes. Do you want details?"

"Definitely not. Just message when you confirm . . . concretely. I don't want details!"

"OK . . . did you want to—"

She cut me off mid-sentence. "Whatever you have to say, message it, and try to answer in a timely fashion," she said, exhaling noisily, clearly annoyed.

"What do you mean?"

"Like I said, I sent you a message not to call . . . that was yesterday. Check your phone."

The line went dead.

Annabelle was being extremely abrupt and rude, but I gave her a pass. She was hurting, and this was a difficult time for her, waiting for the results from my trip to Mexico. I took responsibility; I let it go.

My phone had no new messages, which was odd. Usually I received several messages a day from family and friends, but no one had contacted me since arriving in Mexico. Browsing through the settings, I realized my phone was still on airplane mode. I'd been so preoccupied with my headache, staging and planning, I'd forgotten to remove it.

"Dummy," I scolded myself. After deactivating the setting, several messages were delivered to my phone: a few from my mom, several from my friends, a couple from a blind date disaster who was still looking for a second chance, and one from Annabelle. I clicked on the one from Annabelle. "Do not call. He's watching. Web-based messages only!!!!"

I was happy we'd spoken, despite her complaints. Without explanation, I would have been confused and concerned over her message. Plus, it was clear Annabelle didn't want any reporting structure. Now, feeling relieved things were on track, I decided it was time to freshen up, wanting to wash the tanning oil and chlorine residue off my skin. I smiled to myself, thinking the hotel pools weren't as *natural* as my dad's swimming pool, his dugout. I missed those simple days, swimming with Chloe, not a care in the world . . . now look at me!

After washing off the oil and chemicals, I jumped into bed naked, feeling wonderfully comfortable. My body, surrounded by six large downy pillows, took up half the bed. Looking at my watch, I decided there was time for a nap. I'd been up early. This time I set the alarm.

Chapter 34
Sand Between My Toes

BEEP...BEEP...BEEP...

I woke an hour later to the sound of my alarm. The sheets were so soft I hit snooze—a few short minutes—more loud beeps. I stretched and rolled in the sheets like a playful child, enjoying the softness on my bare skin. It was mid-afternoon, and I still had a few hours before calling Jayson. I wanted to make him wait; it added to the desire. I decided it was time for a workout to freshen my thoughts and burn some calories. I'd consumed a few too many piña coladas earlier that morning, so it was time to equal out my intake/out-take.

Throwing on a pair of short shorts, which barely covered my rear, and a crop top displaying my midriff, I slipped on my sneakers and readied myself for a run. Too lazy to find my brush, I wove my fingers through my hair making a ponytail. I was ready. Glancing at myself in the mirror before leaving, wanting to observe my impromptu ponytail-making skills, I was satisfied. It looked relatively smooth. It would have to do.

Opting out the elevator, which seemed counter-productive, I took the stairs instead and ended up in the hotel lobby. I noticed two runners stretching and prepping for their workout. They had no shoes and were discussing the benefits of running without them. It sounded like a great idea, feeling the sand between my toes. It'd be a nice change.

The clerk at the front desk was accommodating, providing a bin for my shoes. She had several; the idea of running on the beach without footwear had taken off. I started to remove my runners when I felt a tap on my shoulder.

"Excuse me, Miss."

I looked up to find Madoc, who greeted me with his first-class smile. "Hello stranger!" I replied continuing to fiddle with my runners, wondering if our fates were intertwined. We always seemed to end up in the same spot!

"Looks like you had some sun today. I didn't think it was possible, but you look even prettier."

I melted inside but didn't show it. "Aren't you supposed to be at a conference?" I responded, sounding a little too abrupt.

He looked disappointed with my response, then confused. "How did you know I was at a conference?"

Recovering quickly, I found an excuse. "I noticed you were dressed business casual at lunch and didn't see you by the pool all morning, so I could only assume."

The smile returned to his face. "You were looking for me?"

I couldn't help but smirk and nod. "You caught *me* red handed this time." I put my hands up in the air, like he'd done the day before, when we'd first met on the plane.

We looked at each other without saying a word, our gazes glued . . . a sensation locked deep inside started to surface. I pushed it back down. This guy was proving to be too much of a distraction. I needed to get back on task. "Have you seen Jayson?"

His eyes fell and his expression changed to one of disappointment— it seemed to have become a habit with us. "He's not finished with the conference until later today. Our company put together a last-minute information session for senior management regarding concerns over terrorist threats. A guest speaker became available last minute; Jayson falls under the management umbrella, so he had to stay. But if you're looking for company, I'd be happy to fill in."

"I'm fine. Thank you." I was stern, hoping he'd back off, but he had no intention of letting me go that easy.

"I'm not sure why you're so interested in Jayson; we both know he's not your type. Even if you're not interested in me, I care enough about your well-being that I won't rest until you tell me what's up."

His professions of adoration were all too familiar, reminding me of Adam's declaration of love after we'd met. And look how that had turned out! Madoc was stirring up feelings from long ago. I needed to get away from him. I needed to think. I needed to run.

Placing the bin on the concierge desk, I set off for the beach before he could say anything more. I couldn't get away fast enough. Several minutes later my feet hit the hot sand and I welcomed the burning sensation, a distraction from the pain in my heart and the tears running down my cheeks.

Chapter 35
Cupid, stop shooting at me!

WAVES OF EMOTION BOBBED INSIDE MY HEAD. Having Madoc surface in my life caused a plethora of memories to unleash a storm inside my head, like a buoy thrashing this way and that on a stormy night. The healing wounds were becoming exposed again; I ran harder, the sweat pouring down my back.

After Adam, I'd often asked myself how I could have been so far off the mark. I'd thought he loved me—always and forever.

Well . . . always and forever didn't exist anymore. He was gone for good. The hurt had lingered daily for over a year, until it had eventually dissipated; being a good mistress had expedited the healing, but now it was returning to haunt me. I rarely thought of Adam anymore—only when I saw something that reminded me of him, like a fig.

—Fresh figs, my favorite fruit, with their gritty interior filled with crunchy seeds. Their sweetness lingered after every bite. In season only once a year, during the summer months, I'd buy them at least a dozen times before they disappeared off the shelves. The precious treats arrived in the stores packaged in sturdy plastic containers to avoid bruising their delicate flesh.

One summer, I learned an interesting truth about my favorite fruit. It has a cousin fig; not edible, it comes from an ugly, unforgiving tree. Inquiring about the origins of the unusual relative online, I gazed at the computer screen, displaying a lush beautiful tree and, directly beside it, a photo of the same tree after having the misfortune of encountering a fig seed. According to the article, the tropical birds ate figs too and when they defecated on a healthy tree's foliage, any fig seed that grew aggressively, took over the host tree. The issuing woody, woven-like trunk surrounded the tree, eventually suffocating it to death. It's ironic the seeds from such a delicate fruit could metamorphose into such a selfish and hostile tree, the strangler fig; its name an oxymoron.

Adam had been my fig seed. At first, he was sweet, caring, loving, and kind, planting himself into my soul, then he consumed my heart and squeezed the life out of it like the woven trunk of the parasite fig tree—Losing him had caused deep turmoil.

I stopped, forced to rest; huge boulders blocked my path, the beach had ended. I did an about-face, looking for the hotel; it was out of sight. I was satisfied I'd put enough distance between Madoc and me.

Sweat soaked my clothes and a feeling of light-headedness swept over me. Dehydration. I'd left in such haste I'd forgotten a water bottle. Extremely hot and sweaty, I waded into the ocean, the cool water welcoming against my warm skin. Diving into the approaching waves, I tasted the salt water on my lips. I played in the ocean, momentarily allowing myself to revert to childhood. Returning to the beach to lie on the sand, I let the waves lap over my toes. I was deep in thought meditating.

It was clear I hadn't quite recovered yet—the tears being the proof. For over a year, I'd worn protective armor, escaping Cupid's arrows, eluding love, or so I'd thought. And then Madoc appeared in my life, testing me. Cupid was shooting at me again! He turned out to be mightier than me, his large arrow piercing my rock-hard barrier, managing to find my Achilles' heel. My heart was being won over despite my best efforts. I didn't think it would have been possible to fall in love again after Adam, but it was happening, Madoc was a contender.

My run had provided a new perspective on Madoc. His timely meeting had unearthed the leftover, hidden feelings inside me. As the waves continued to lap at my toes, I started to piece together a theory as to why I was still suffering from a broken heart . . . I had closed myself off to love.

Love was a basic human need and by denying it, I hadn't been able to fully heal. But was I willing to fall in love again? Love was messy. I wasn't sure which was worse: not allowing myself to love or suffering the possibility of another broken heart. My mind was flailing again, like a fish out of water. My thoughts were coming fast and floundering inside my head. *What is love, anyhow? Can it even be defined? It means so many different things to so many different people. What does love mean to me?*

Love for me, this time, would involve a healthy, respect-ful, committed relationship with someone who was *avail-able*, someone who wasn't married.

I was no longer the fragile woman from a year ago, having become invincible like the punching clown I'd played with as a kid. The clown was fearless and strong. Every time I playfully punched, its bouncy body would lean backward, only to return quickly to its original position. The clown's face was forever smiling, taunting me to punch him again, which I did over and over. And it always came back up. I had become the inflatable clown during my recovery, taking the painful relationship punches and learning to absorb them, feel them, and best of all, learn from them. I'd remained upright and smiling, despite all life's punches.

The waves were receding, the tide going out, and I watched a woman in her mid-forties pass by with her partner. They strolled hand in hand, appearing serene and content. She looked like my mother and I was reminded of a late-night call I'd placed to her shortly after Adam and I were no longer together. I'd been seeking solace.

"Bree, you need to put these sad feelings into a box and store it way, deep inside you, never to be found again." Ice cubes rattled in her glass as she took a long sip. "Yup! As deep as you can!" She'd taken up drinking vodka and cran-berry most nights since she'd found out my dad was sexting with the neighbor. He hadn't physically cheated on her, but she was scarred nonetheless after reading the provocative messages between the two of them. She'd created her own box, thinking she had the ability to stuff it all away, like it'd never happened. But all the nasty feelings festered inside—rotting in some dark corner.

I'd taken Mom's advice at first but soon realized it wasn't helping, so I'd opened the box, peered deep inside, and dismantled it piece by piece, day by day, steering my rowboat to calmer waters. No matter how hard it hurt, no matter how much I cried, and no matter how many times I had to open that damn box, I'd opened it, and now, just when I'd thought it was empty, Madoc had stirred up those old feelings. Luckily, I was practised at managing pain and instead of leaving those feelings untreated, like Mom, I was dealing with them as I soaked up the sun's rays.

The second and last time I'd spoken with my mother about Adam was a week later. I'd called again, having another bad day—they were frequent back then. Her voice was accusatory as I cried into the phone. "Your dad did the same thing to me. I loved and respected your father, but he turned my world upside down when he decided to cheat on me. I don't care if it was just sexting. It's still cheating. Now, you and this man have done the same thing to his wife. I told your father to stay away from her. I could see plain as day she was trouble, coming around in her low-cut shirts, asking your father to help her fix something at her house. I didn't even think your father wanted sex anymore. We haven't had sex since . . ."

Interrupting her, not wanting to hear about their sex life, I pleaded, "Please Mom. I don't want to know details about *that* stuff."

"Fine!" she complained in a gruff voice, and then carried on about the evils of cheating.

I suddenly lost my patience. "Well, maybe if you had paid some attention to Dad, he would never have cheated."

She gasped, and I regretted saying it. There was a long silence, which was unusual. She always had a lot to say, but I'd apparently flabbergasted her with my comment. "While I'm sorry *you* feel that way, I am *sure* your father thinks otherwise."

Dad was a pushover and only told Mom what she wanted to hear, so I wouldn't be getting any backup from him. "I'm sorry, Mom. It was rude of me. I'm just making excuses for my behavior."

"Yes, you are. Now stop sulking and get over him. I didn't shed a tear when I found out your dad had cheated on me."

That's because you have no feelings, I wanted to say, but this time I kept my thoughts to myself. My mother was too stubborn to listen to anything I had to say anyhow. She started in again, lecturing about the immoralities of cheating, when suddenly her voice trailed off and her breathing picked up. Sounding panicked, she angrily shouted, "She's here!" She was seething. "How dare she walk by my house with her big saggy tits hanging out? I'm going to make sure those tits never come around here again." She hung up without saying good-bye.

Despite knowing love had dwindled from their marriage, death by a thousand cuts, just like Annabelle and Jayson's marriage, it still hurt to know my dad had cheated emotionally on my mom. I'd come to realize Mom loved me but was unable to support me. Her husband cheated on her, so she had no sympathy for a daughter who had done the same to another woman—she was right.

I'd consoled myself that night with cookie dough ice cream and with the notion most relationships turned out like my mother and father's anyhow, partnerships of convenience. I reasoned Adam and I would most likely have turned out like my parents. I knew steadfast love took time, understanding, patience, and kindness . . . and we would never have arrived there with a ring on his finger.

Without my mom to support me, I turned to a close friend with a sympathetic ear, Sophia. We'd known each other since high school. She was wise for her years and always listened, having a knack at giving good advice. The affectionate nickname I bestowed upon her was "the owl."

One day, needing to talk, I invited her out for lunch. Anxious to receive her wisdom, I arrived at our favorite shawarma place half an hour before the rendezvous. I had so much I wanted to tell her.

She walked through the doors twenty minutes later, her smiling face turning to a frown at the sight of the dark circles bordering my red puffy eyes. Relieved to see her, wanting to unburden my sorrows, I'd poured out my concerns before her bottom could hit the chair. She listened as I unleashed. I was having second thoughts about the night I caught Adam with another woman—Maybe Adam's co-worker had only answered his hotel room phone because everyone had gone back to his hotel for drinks? —Maybe I should call him?

I was a mess and desperately wanted to hear his voice again, even if it meant contradicting common sense. I was frustrated, wanting answers—Why had he given up so easily? —Why wasn't he chasing me like before? Surely I should have heard from him since the day he'd knocked at my door! —Had I chased him away when I'd threatened to tell his wife? —Did he really believe I would do such a thing? It had been a veiled threat; he should have known that!

She let me rant for over an hour without saying much until I specifically asked her, "Is he coming back?"

Without hesitation, without consideration, she answered, "No."

I didn't realize the pain could be even more acute; my heart sank to an even deeper, darker level than I had ever imagined possible. It was then I realized my little owl was right . . . he wasn't coming back.

In my heart of hearts, I knew he was gone. He was not the man I had made him out to be. He was running for his life like a mouse being chased by a cat, fearful his wife would find out—What happened to the kind, humble, and caring man I'd fallen in love with? —Had I just imagined him into life, fooling myself into believing he existed?

The man I had dreamed into existence would not have run like a coward, but instead would have taken me into his arms and told me everything was going to be OK.

The rest of the night, we talked about safer subjects, like her kids and my job, but it was all a blur. I was in a trance, void of any emotion.

Although I knew she was right, I secretly longed for my owl to be wrong…just this once. I checked my phone constantly but still nothing! Although I'd changed my number, he would surely have sought it out from the owner at the

Chic Chick, making the excuse he'd misplaced it. I came up with a million ways for him to find me; he never did.

Shaking my phone, prompting it to work, trying to force a message from Adam never worked. Most of the time, I didn't know if I should cry or laugh at myself, embarrassed by my behavior. For almost a year, I checked my phone several times a day, hoping to hear from him, but gradually I stopped checking, and then I finally gave up.

After meeting Madoc, I was starting to believe it wasn't that I missed Adam so much as I missed being in love.

On the enlightening thought, I got up, making my way back to the hotel. I felt happier then I'd been in a long time. I had so many things in my life to be grateful for: friends, family and now, possibly, a new man. With their help, I'd been able to build a sturdy brick emotional house—no longer made of hay or twigs. My solid-brick home meant I could take a lot more huffing and puffing if Madoc ever turned out to be a big bad wolf!

My thoughts were disturbed by a seagull screaming up above, circling the ocean, looking for its next meal; the noisy creature reminding me it was almost dinner time and I still had to prepare for my evening with Jayson. Not wanting to miss another opportunity to connect with him, I considered some additional trepidations. *What about Madoc?* I would eventually have to explain my actions to him, without exposing Annabelle. I wasn't sure how to solve the issue yet, but it was the least of my concerns…for the time being.

Needing to get ready, I started to jog, reaching the hotel in good time. Smiling when I arrived, a stark difference from when I left, I was ready to take on the evening!

Chapter 36
Sex Is Like a Box of Chocolates . . .

TAKING THE TIME TO ADMIRE THE PRISTINE landscape of the hotel on the way to the reception area I marveled at green manicured lawns, fountains trickling, and an abundance of fruit hanging from the trees, ripe for picking and ready for consumption at the buffets. I hadn't taken the time to admire it upon my arrival, preoccupied with my headache and Jayson. *Paradise*, I thought, approaching the front desk, wiping the sand off my feet before entering the main lobby— a courtesy to the cleaning staff.

Taking a scan of the area for Madoc, looking this way and that, I searched for any signs of him; there were none. My protector had retreated from his duties for the time being.

Suddenly and unexpectedly a sexual urge flowed through me; I wanted Madoc, badly. I stood thinking, hoping he was great in bed, like expensive, high-quality chocolate. My expectations had reached an all-new high with Adam. I remember telling my friend Sophia I couldn't go back to the hook ups; Smarties sex. Sure, it was good, cheap, and easy to find, like Smarties at every corner store, but Swedish chocolate, the fancy meaningful sex with someone you love, was harder to find and much more rewarding. I was ready for some 'Swedish chocolate'—right now—in the hotel lobby! My sexual drive was in full gear as I reached the front counter, thinking about how surprised Madoc would be with my change of heart if I pulled him into the lobby elevators to let him have his way with me. I reasoned, I still had to finish my job with Jayson—business before pleasure.

In my limited Spanish, I greeted the receptionist, "*Buenos días, señorita.*"

"Good day," she replied in English, not in her native tongue as I'd hoped.

Perhaps my Spanish needs some work? I made a mental note to sign up for some Spanish lessons when I arrived home. Then retrieving my runners, I asked for a bottle of water, in English.

I found a bench near the elevators and sat down. The air conditioning was doing its job; the metal was cool on my warm skin. Opening the bottle of water and finishing it within seconds, I revived. My runners had been wiped clean, thanks to the staff. I was impressed. Slipping my right foot into my footwear, I felt a rough object touch my toes and I jumped, quickly withdrawing my foot. I reprimanded myself, knowing better than to put my foot inside without checking; tropical insects were always in search of dark places. Tilting my runner toward the light to get a better look I was relieved to see a piece of paper.

I pulled out the culprit as a concierge walked my way. "I'm so sorry, Señorita Bree! You received an urgent message. I didn't mean to startle you."

Looking upset, he fidgeted, like a nervous chicken searching for her babies. Placing my hand on his arm, I reassured him, "At least, I'll remember to check my shoes next time! *Gracias, mi amigo.*"

"*De nada, señorita!*" He beamed, pleasing me with a Spanish response. A service bell rang in the distance, and he began fidgeting once more, heading back to his post.

Curious, I unfolded the note. The message was handwritten on the hotel's stationery, probably by the concierge. Underneath the hotel's logo, it was written:

Talk to Madoc ASAP

Annabelle

Chapter 37
Knock. Knock.

ANNABELLE KNEW MADOC? *OF COURSE*, I THOUGHT. Madoc was her husband's co-pilot. But why did she leave a message with the front desk and not contact my phone? I moaned, remembering I'd left my phone on the charger in my room. Bounding up the stairs, two by two, I wondered what this could possibly be about. Arriving quickly in my room, I went straight for my phone. Five missed calls and a message, all from Annabelle. Unable to reach me, she'd sent a message, all in caps: STAND DOWN. TALK TO MADOC. ROOM 221.

I was confused; what had happened during the time I had gone for a run? Suddenly, feeling faint from the heat and fluid loss, I realized my state of dehydration. The one bottle of water had not compensated for the loss of water I'd sustained. Needing more, I took a frosty bottle from the mini fridge, gulping it back. The chilled water ran down my throat, cooling my insides. Some of the liquid had managed to escape the corners of my mouth while I'd been chugging the goods like a cavewoman. Wiping my chin, I took note of my reflection in the mirror: a hot sweaty mess, in need of a cleanup before seeking out Madoc.

I ran my bath, keeping the water tepid, then slipped into the tub. The water spilled around me, cleaning and cooling my hot sticky skin. My headache was dissolving. Breathing in deeply, I concentrated on the water around me. The bath soap had formed large bubbles and carried the soft scent of peaches. The water poured generously into the tub, covering every inch of my body, soothing me.

After twenty minutes, I'd cooled sufficiently, and the bubbles were starting to go flat. I let the water seep out, feeling it tug against my body as the drain greedily drank it up. Now, headache free, I was anxious to get out of the tub. I needed to find Madoc. How did he fit into this puzzle?

Stepping out of the tub, then reaching for a towel, I dabbed at my hair and body, patting it dry.

A friendly double knock sounded at the door. It had to be Maria, the maid. We'd chatted earlier in the hallway. She had six children with a seventh on the way, her belly large and growing day by day. Having little money, she continued to work, and her nightly duties included turn-down service; she'd mentioned stopping by later.

My long, wet hair was dripping on the floor, making a mess, but I didn't want to leave her waiting, so I wrapped the bath towel around my body and opened the door.

Maria, it was not!

Chapter 38
Keeping Score

"WELL, HELLO, SUGAR!" JAYSON PURRED. "I SEE you're already *wet* for me, I like it," he mused, running his fingers through my sopping hair, laughing, entertained by his play on words. "That's a great start." Staggering forward a little, smelling of alcohol, he leaned in for a kiss.

In shock, mouth ajar, I obliged, wondering how he'd found my room. I hadn't given him the number, yet there he was, drunk at my door.

Still in shock, putting my hand on his chest, I pulled away, hoping to stop his affections. "How did you know where to find me, hun?"

Taking my words as an invitation, he forged his way into the room. "I have my ways. They like me around here. I stay at this hotel often and tip well. I couldn't stop thinking about how sweet you must taste," he said, smacking his lips at the thought, "so I tracked down your room number, and voilà, here I am!"

Kicking the door shut with his left foot, managing to keep his balance this time, he fastened the latch, sealing us in the room. He was blocking the doorway like a hungry bear who'd just wakened from hibernation.

Jayson was prepared for the occasion, a fancy wine bottle in hand, and dressed nicely: golf shirt and plaid shorts, with a sweater wrapped around his shoulders, tied in front, Ken and Barbie style. I had to admit he looked considerably handsome.

"Were you golfing?" I queried, trying to divert his thoughts from anything sexual. Adjusting the sweater on his shoulders, he nodded. He'd obviously just come from the hotel's nearby golf course, which provided unlimited top shelf drinks.

Moving in my direction, waving the bottle of wine in front of my face, he grinned. "Let's get this party started."

My feeble attempt at distraction was failing miserably. Being clothed simply in a towel wasn't helping either!

"Looks expensive!" I nodded approvingly, eyeballing the bottle of wine.

I'd left my phone in the bathroom and my mind was frantically looking for an excuse to get to it, needing to contact Annabelle to get some clarification on what she wanted me to do. The lion had come to feast. Should I let him? She'd asked me to see Madoc before proceeding and I needed to find out why!

"Why don't you open the bottle of wine? Let it breathe a little while I get into something a little more comfortable."

Moving in closer, taking me by the waist, he breathed, "Baby what you have on is okay by me. Besides we don't want anything covering that fine-looking body of yours anyhow."

As he nudged in for another kiss, I squirmed, slipping out of his reach. "Now, now. I need a little wine to get things started. A little wine goes a long way with me."

Dipping behind the bathroom door, I playfully tossed my towel in his direction. "I'll only be a moment."

I shut the door, locked it, and grabbed my phone. Then I waited until I heard Jayson rummaging through the mini bar, most likely looking for some glasses. My fingers shook as I dialed his wife's number; thankfully, she answered on the first ring.

"Annabelle, what's happening? He's in my room," I whispered.

"Who? Madoc?" she probed.

"No, your husband!" I exclaimed.

She gasped, and I heard her take in a deep breath. She tried to talk, but her voice cracked as she obviously fought back tears.

"Unfortunately, you were right." I didn't try to ease the burden of my words. There wasn't much time!

"I know," she cried.

I paused, puzzled. *Why had she sent me to Mexico if she knew he was cheating?*

"I don't understand," I murmured into the phone. "You need to explain this, and quickly."

"I got an unexpected call from Madoc! He was out of sorts...he had something to tell me... his explanation started with you! He'd met a beautiful woman by the name of Bree, and was falling for her! He realized immediately you were special. I've known Madoc for a decade and he doesn't fall in love easily."

She stopped, catching her breath. "Anyhow he was calling because he wanted to protect you from my husband, and to make a long story short…he told me about Jayson's affairs. Jayson had told him we were in an open relationship, swingers! He was beginning to suspect it wasn't the case, so he called me." Her words came tumbling out. "I told him everything, the whole truth . . . about you, Jayson, and Mexico! That's when he remembered the score sheet!"

Tap, tap, tap.

I jumped.

"Baby the wine can't wait any longer and neither can I."

Covering the mouth piece of my phone, in the sexiest voice I could muster despite the circumstances, I cooed, "Baby the wait is worth it. I'll be out in less than a minute, I promise."

My head was spinning, and I wanted to ask her about Madoc. What did he think about all of this? But, there was no time. I had her horny husband waiting for me on the other side of the bathroom door.

"What do you mean a score sheet? Be clearer!" It was my turn to be rude, annoyed she'd told Madoc about my antics.

"That was *him,* wasn't it? That bastard! How could he do this to our family?"

"Annabelle, I need you to focus. What score sheet?"

I could almost feel her back straighten and her voice became calm again. "Jayson calls it his score sheet. He's bragged to Madoc about it. He uses a ledger to keep track of the women he's had sex with, rating them based on their looks and sexual performance. How juvenile! Madoc felt terrible; he wished he had known and told me sooner. And guess what? I found it, hidden under a floorboard in Sadie's room," she declared triumphantly then paused and drew out a long breath. "There were a lot of names in the ledger and he even had the nerve to rate me, his own wife!"

"I'm so sorry, Annabelle," I said sorrowfully, making her the priority.

"At least the late nights of wondering and the anxiety of not knowing are finally over. Now I know what I've suspected for a long time. I tried to call you several times, but you never answered, so I called the front desk, leaving a message. Madoc wanted to fill you in on everything."

BANG, BANG, BANG! His knocks were getting louder, and more impatient.

"Who are you talking to in there?"

Trying to open the door, he impatiently rattled the handle. Luckily, I'd locked it.

"How are you going to get rid of my husband?" Annabelle whispered as if he might hear.

"Easy peasy. I'll just kick him out." I sighed, relieved I didn't have to get messy with Jayson. His wife already had all the proof she needed. I'd have to sort things out with Madoc later, but for now I needed to get rid of Jayson.

"Ok, what's your room number, so Madoc can find you?"

"541. I have to go."

Clicking the end button, I grabbed the hotel bathrobe hanging on the back of the door and put it on. This time, I was clothed and ready to face Jayson. Opening the door, I gawked in surprise. Jayson was standing outside the door completely naked, his erection at attention.

Stepping through the doorway I squeezed my way past him, taking ground three feet away. He still had the bottle of wine in hand, only now it was three quarters empty.

"Hey! —not what I expected . . . from a towel to a bathrobe? Better be something nice underneath." He looked displeased with my choice of clothing. "Let's see what you have for Jayson underneath all the cotton. Now, come here, baby." He tugged at the rope holding my bathrobe shut.

How did this man get so many women to sleep with him? — It was a mystery. I backed away, but his firm grip on the rope caused my bathrobe to come undone, exposing my breasts.

"Whoa! That's some rack you have!" He nodded approvingly, advancing. I put up my palm, like a police officer stopping traffic.

Thinking quickly, needing an excuse to call it off, it came to me; I was going to use my make-believe boyfriend as a way out. Jayson thought I'd come to Mexico to get over a break up—the perfect angle. "I changed my mind, my boyfriend called. That's who I was talking to... he wants me back, so this changes things. I'm out!"

"You changed your mind, did you? I think you're just playing hard to get again."

As he reached for my exposed breasts, I was able to shield him off, closing my bathrobe shut, gripping the robe firmly with both hands in case he tried again. This guy wasn't going to be as easy to get rid of as I'd thought.

Jayson stood looking at me in disbelief, probably trying to decide if I was teasing or serious. He tipped the bottle of wine to his lips, finishing it off with several large gulps before dropping it to the ground. Licking the excess wine from his lips, he eye-balled me, his gaze glazed and lustful. I didn't like the way he was leering at me. He wasn't about to take no for an answer.

"Hun, I have to get something from the bathroom," I said, trying to put a locked door between us again—looking for refuge—but before I could, he grabbed the shoulder of my bathrobe and pulled it off entirely. We were both naked now, standing inches from each other. Wanting cover, I tried to screen my breasts with my hands. "Now that's better. Why so shy suddenly? There is no reason to be hiding those great tits. Besides those small hands of yours barely cover half." He chortled heartily at his own joke.

A fury rose inside me at his disgusting, aggressive behavior.

"You need to leave! Now!" I pointed to the door, freeing one hand, exposing a breast.

His gaze fixed on my breast, his eyes dark. "Stop playing hard to get, baby," he seethed. "Believe me, you're going to like it."

Grabbing himself again, he flicked his cock against my thigh as if trying to prove his point.

I backed away, not getting far.

With his other hand, he grabbed a handful of hair and forced me to the ground, so I was level with his groin. I couldn't believe it! I was in the exact same position I had been with Evan—I knew exactly what to do. Although this time I'd be using a different twist.

Attempting to guide his sex toward my mouth, he demanded, "Just have a taste."

"I'd love to!" I opened my mouth, ready to bite down hard. Seeing what I was about to do, he pulled away, pushing me backward. My head hit the floor and I cried out in pain.

"You, crazy bitch!" he fumed, coming toward me again. I had expected him to curl into a ball like Evan, but this guy was smarter and faster than Evan. "I didn't realize you liked it rough!"

Lying on the ground with my head throbbing, glimpses of my dream flashed before my eyes. The girl...the axe... the helpless kitten . . . it had indeed been a warning, but I'd chosen to ignore it.

Feeling faint and dizzy, I knew I had to figure out my next line of defence. The hotel had thin walls; I'd heard the honeymooners making love in the room beside me. If I screamed, someone would hear me. But before I had the chance, Jayson's large hand clamped across my mouth—the smell of his penis and the taste of salty sweat—I gagged.

Now he was on top of me and I could feel his hardness resting on my leg. I struggled, but he was much stronger, easily pinning me to the floor with his body weight. I bit into the flesh on his arm, but he didn't even flinch; it only aroused him more.

"Keep biting! I like it rough too!" He started to move in closer, so I fought harder, to no avail. He whispered something into my ear and a wicked smile spread across his face. The words barely registered. My head felt light. It was getting dark . . .

Chapter 39
Karma

BANG! BANG! BANG!

"Bree! It's Madoc. Is everything all right in there?" I could hear the distress in his voice.

Jayson immediately jumped off, looking startled, then angry for being disturbed.

I started to answer but was cut off by Jayson.

"What are you doing here, Madoc?"

"Open the door Jayson! You're drunk," Madoc snarled, continuing to bang forcibly, the door shaking under the weight of his fists.

"Didn't realize you liked her so much!"

Jayson grabbed my bathrobe off the ground, using it to cover himself, and opened the door wide. "Well, come on in. You can have her, then." He bowed to Madoc and gestured in my direction.

"What did you do, Jayson?" Madoc looked at me in horror; I was lying on the floor, naked. He rushed to my side as I clutched the back of my aching head.

"She likes it rough. What can I say?" He winked at Madoc, walked over to the bed, and started whistling while he dressed.

Madoc helped me up. "Are you OK, Bree? Did he . . . did he hurt you? Because if he did, so help me." He clenched his fists, his voice shaking with anger.

"It could have been worse, but you're here now, thankfully."

Madoc helped me to the bathroom and I sat on the edge of the tub. Covering me with a towel, he tilted my head upward, studying my eyes. "I need to check for a concussion."

We heard the door. Jayson was letting himself out. "Oh, by the way, Madoc, be careful. That one likes to bite." He roared like a lion, then slammed the door shut.

Madoc clenched his fists and turned towards the door. "I'm going to beat the shit out of him."

"Please don't! Stop!" I held onto his arm, trying to steady him, but my pleas were falling on deaf ears. Madoc was seeing red. He'd taken care of me first but now he looked ready to take care of Jayson! I could feel the pressure mounting inside my head, the pain was so intense I began to moan. Letting go of his arm, I grasped the back of my head.

Madoc instantly re-focused his efforts onto me, sweeping me into his arms and carrying me to the bed. "You need to sleep. If the headache is still there when you wake up, I'm taking you to the doctor."

I was happy he'd chosen to care for me over giving Jayson an old school beat down. I didn't want to drag Madoc any further into the situation. He'd already helped enough.

Besides, we'd be having the last laugh after Jayson returned home to his wife, score sheet in hand. I knew from experience karma had a way of working things out.

He fussed over me, wrapping the blankets around my body, taking care, being delicate and kind, as if he were tucking in a child. But all the while he mumbled to himself—when he saw Jayson again he'd beat him good.

I lay there in shock, concerned Madoc would go after Jayson once I was asleep. I was even more concerned with Madoc's perception of me. What did he think had just happened? What did he think of me? I wanted to tell him everything. I was desperate to explain why he'd found us naked. I wanted to tell him I'd been completely reckless—he was right. He'd warned me and I hadn't listened. I started speaking, the words coming out jumbled.

He placed his finger on my lips. "Sleep, Bree! Sleep! I'll watch over you. We can talk later, once you've rested. I'm not leaving you, *ever*."

My body was exhausted, so I didn't protest. Closing my eyes, I could feel the warmth of Madoc's body as he sat by my side, comforting me . . . I knew everything was going to be all right. I was safe!

Chapter 40
Full Circle

I WOKE TO THE SUN SEEPING INTO MY ROOM, RAYS of sunshine on my face. I was sleepy but at least my head didn't hurt. Clearing the fog from my eyes, I immediately looked for Madoc: *where was he?* My heart sank. He'd come to his senses and changed his mind. I could hardly blame him. Relationships were hard enough without having a partner who was a mistress for hire. Although, after my experience with Jayson, I was considering a career change. I curled into a ball, suddenly feeling cold despite the heat, and covered myself with the sheets.

I didn't want Madoc to give up on me; I needed to show him it could work. I started to consider my next move; I was going to win him over.

I heard movement at the foot of the bed. Startled, I sat up and the sheets fell to my waist. Still naked from the night before, I peered over the foot of the bed and there he was, fast asleep on the floor, still in his clothes from the previous day. He didn't even have a blanket to ease his rest.

Elated and overjoyed he'd stayed, I longed for him more than ever. Quietly getting out of bed I knelt beside him, taking in and appreciating his many features. He was ruggedly handsome with his thick light brown hair, square jaw, and muscular arms. I slipped my hand under his shirt and he woke suddenly, looking worried.

"Are you OK? Sorry I fell asleep." He hadn't yet noticed I was naked, but his eyes quickly fell to my chest. "We need to get you back in bed. I'm not convinced you want to do this. You may be injured and not thinking straight."

"Madoc, I have no headache, no injuries. Just a complete desire to have you inside me."

He didn't argue. Taking me into his arms, he carried me to bed like he had the night before, this time for a different purpose.

Lying in bed as we trailed our fingers along each other's bodies, he smiled, his expression soft and sweet. His movements were slow... deliberate. His eyes took in every inch of my nakedness.

Stilling his hand, his smile now playful, he confessed, "I hadn't expected to end up here this morning. Aren't I a lucky man? —Beside the most beautiful woman in the world."

I blushed at his compliment, not saying anything, at loss for words and happy to finally have him in my bed.

Running the back of his hand along my cheek, he locked eyes with me. I felt like he was looking right into me, into my soul. He leaned in, kissing me deeply, lovingly. I returned his affections, pressing into him, lusting for him to be inside me. I slid over him, wanting to be on top, and he eased into me. I slowly pushed back and forth, looking into his eyes.

He reached for my hands, not taking his eyes off mine, intertwining our fingers. I rode him gently at first, enjoying the sensation. He felt so good I soon moved faster and harder. Grinding into me, he found the right spot over and over. Each of his thrusts brought me closer and closer. I moaned, ready.

Reading each other, we knew we were both nearing the edge. On his final thrust, we finished together, our eyes still locked.

We lay tangled in the crisp white sheets, staring at the ceiling. He cradled my head in his arms as he ran a hand through my long hair. Not saying a word, enjoying the moment, we fell asleep in each other's arms, spent and happy. We woke a short while later to do it all again.

We made love all morning, then again in the afternoon, until our bodies were depleted. After exploring our physical side, we tended to the emotional. I told Madoc everything he wanted to know about Brody, Evan, and Jayson and the three women I'd helped during my short stint as a mistress for hire. He listened and nodded with few questions. He understood why I'd chosen my unusual career path, saying it was a noble cause, but hoped I'd think about choosing another path, one less dangerous. He didn't want to discuss it any more than that.

Lying in bed for hours, we continued to talk, this time about our families, friends, aspirations, and dreams. As we toyed with the idea of leaving the room to go for supper, I ran my fingers over a scar on his upper left forehead; it looked considerably faded, an old wound, but still noticeable. I kissed it. "May I ask what happened here?"

"Oh, that. My prize bull bucked me straight off and into a metal fence post. The damage was fifteen stiches, two weeks of headaches, and an end to my riding career. Hence why I was so concerned about you having a concussion. I've had more than I can count."

I listened intently, intrigued, as he talked about the old bull getting the better of him and his grandpa getting the better of the old bull—shooting the poor animal in the forehead with a .22 rifle. My mouth formed a startled O; I was taken by surprise by his grandpa's actions.

Madoc read my expression. "That was the way on the farm, Bree. Doesn't mean I didn't feel responsible for the bull's death, even though he'd ended my riding career."

My heart fluttered with affection as I listened to his explanation.

"I didn't agree with my Grandpa. It was wrong what he did. The bull was only doing what it had been bred to do. But I know Grandpa loved me, and I understand why he'd acted out of anger."

My heart was growing fonder by the minute. I laid my head on his chest and my hand on his heart. I could hear his heartbeat thumping in my ear; it warmed me. His stomach growled. I realized we had forgotten to eat lunch, being so pre-occupied with each other!

We ordered in, deciding to stay within the confines of my room so we could continue to indulge in each other. My love life had come full circle, without warning, and I was more than happy to go along for the ride.

Chapter 41
See You Later, Alligator. In a While, Crocodile.

THE NEXT MORNING, I AWOKE IN HIS ARMS, HEAD ON his chest, a position I was growing fond of—I was in heaven. The smell of his sweet cologne filled my senses and his heartbeat pulsated in my ear, a lullaby beckoning me back to sleep. Resisting the temptation, I lifted my head to study him while he slept.

His thick silky hair summoned me, imploring my fingers to run through the short strands. Madoc moaned at my touch. His gorgeous eyes opened, gazing at me intently. He was ruggedly handsome. A shadow of facial hair had spread across his firm jawline, only making him sexier.

A sly smile appeared on my lips as I pondered for a beat. *The moment is perfect. He's perfect.* Lust built inside me. I bit my bottom lip in anticipation.

He looked at me—at my eyes, my mouth; I could almost see him thinking. He leaned in and we kissed, long, hard, and deep, our tongues finding each other. I was completely aroused and could have climaxed just as we were. I'd never been so turned on in my life. I never wanted the feeling to end.

We were still naked from the day before. Clothes only got in our way. Anxious to have him inside me, I turned over and nestled my bottom into his groin, rubbing it back and forth over his hardness. I gasped as his fullness entered me. He reached from behind and wrapped his arms tightly around me—I was his captive.

He thrust into me, running his hands over my breasts, in between my legs, and then finally resting on either side on my hips. He plunged deeper into me.

On the edge, I closed my eyes, not wanting to lose my mind; the feeling was so intense. Then, with one final thrust, I screamed his name as he lightly bit into my shoulder.

Our bodies shuddered, and the warmth of our orgasms filled us. We lay together, bound by his erectness. Several moments later, he withdrew and we fell deeper into the covers. He wrapped me in his arms again and we lay together, not saying a word, not needing to . . . the moment was forever perfect.

We fell asleep again and woke an hour later. After making love a second time, we cuddled the rest of the morning, then finally decided to expand our horizons and set out on an excursion. Madoc was free for the rest of his stay. He had advised the conference facilitator he was unable to attend the rest of the conference and was willing to reimburse the company for their loss. The facilitator agreed, and Madoc was free to enjoy the rest of his stay alongside his new lady. We weren't concerned about running into Jayson, as karma had found him during a phone call with his wife. Annabelle texted me to say Jayson was taking the next flight home and she thanked both Madoc and I for our help.

A dozen guests lingered in front of the hotel, waiting for the tour guide to arrive. According to the brochure, his name was Juan. The day had already grown hot and many guests were already fanning themselves, anxious for the arrival of the air-conditioned safari bus.

It pulled up early, an open-sided Jeep with a simple tarp covering the roof. No air conditioning for us, but I wasn't about to complain. I had everything I needed right beside me. I wrapped my arms around Madoc's neck. Then, leaning on my tippy toes, I reached his cheek, planting a big fat kiss.

"What was that for?" He looked pleased.

"For being you." I beamed, smiling foolishly, looking completely in love.

Our eyes locked and lingered, oblivious to the people around us. I smiled broadly, realizing we'd met my definition of love.

The driver impatiently beeped his horn—we were the only ones who hadn't boarded his vehicle, not noticing the other passengers had already gone ahead of us. We chose the only seats left, at the front of the bus, quickly settling in before being disciplined again. Instinctively, I reached for a seatbelt, but as per Mexican standards, or lack thereof, no seatbelts were to be found.

We enjoyed the entire, snuggled into each other like long-lost lovers. Several passengers glanced our way and smiled. The warm wind brushed against our faces and the sun soaked into our skin. I was the happiest I'd ever been, but for some reason I momentarily thought of Adam! It was the first time I'd thought of him since being with Madoc. But it was a pleasant thought—my memories were like ashes turned to diamonds. I smiled, thinking all my experiences with Adam and being a mistress for hire had brought me to this point...to Madoc. I looked over at him, who lovingly gazed back at me.

The bus pulled up to a parking area near a waterfall and Juan hollered for us to exit the bus. Previously being in the hospitality service, I deduced he didn't make many tips with his straightforward approach. Or perhaps he was just having a bad day. Regardless, I was feeling over the moon and prepared to give him a generous tip. We all filed out, one by one, like soldiers marching to his commands. In broken English, he explained we had exactly one hour, not a minute more. He pointed to the waterfall, again commanding us to make our way over. The group moved toward the falls in unison, like sheep being herded to pasture.

I took in my surroundings. The falls were breath-taking and the water cascaded off the moss-covered rocks into a large pool of pristine water. The lush forest thrived off the humidity provided by the falls and the whole area looked picturesque, a postcard.

Jogging to the first picnic table I could see, I hastily slipped off my sun dress. We only had one hour! I had a turquoise bikini underneath, which complimented the color of my surroundings.

"First one to the falls wins." I squealed in excitement, jumping into the water before Madoc had even had a chance to remove his sandals. Determined to make it to the falls before him, I feverishly paddled my limbs, but he was strong and incredibly athletic and caught up to me in no time. He playfully passed me, then slowed down, letting me take the lead. We found a smaller waterfall and treaded water beneath it, enjoying the natural massage nature was providing. After a few minutes of pampering, we swam underneath, and rested on a small platform submerged near the bottom. It made for a nice ledge to stand on.

"Thanks for letting me win, handsome. Why did you do that?"

"Because I was hoping you'd like to claim me as your prize." He kissed me softly and I enjoyed the mixture of tastes—his sweet lips and the fresh water.

The waterfall streamed over us, we continued to kiss; blissfully content. The smell of coconut filled the air as our suntan lotion washed off around us.

As Madoc nibbled at my ear, I saw a young mother eyeing us disapprovingly, tugging at her son, who was pointing our way, looking at us with curiosity. We tucked ourselves farther behind the waterfall to ensure more privacy. We hadn't had sex in over two hours and the tension was already building. I could feel him growing harder against my leg as my scantily clad breasts rubbed against his chest. He slipped my bikini bottom to the side and I moaned in anticipation.

The sudden panicked cries of the 'muchacho' disrupted the moment.

"*Cocodrilo! Cocodrilo! Cocodrilo!*"

My back tensed. Not wanting to alarm Madoc, I didn't say a word but thought, *I don't speak much Spanish but that sure sounds like crocodile!* Looking at the concern in Madoc's eyes, I knew he was thinking the same.

Pausing our indiscretions, we peeked our heads through the waterfall. The curious boy, who had just been pointing at us was now pointing to a large crocodile, about seventy-five feet away.

The scaly creature was on a shoreline, separate from the picnic area, but sharing the same waterfront. Without saying a word, Madoc defensively placed himself in front of me, and we began to slowly swim toward the shore. I glanced around, noticing we were the only ones who had made it so far into the water.

Juan began to usher the passengers toward the bus. He hadn't taken notice of us, tucked in behind the falls, but the crocodile's keen eyes had, and they were fixed on us as the creature started to wade into the water. I began to panic; Madoc reached back and placed his hand firmly on my waist. "We got this, babe. You're safe. I won't let anything happen to you. Don't make any sudden movements, just swim quickly but calmly and look at the bus. It will help you stay focused." His voice was soothing.

I felt safe. I knew he wouldn't let anything happen—just like he had done with Jayson.

I glanced over to the shore, the 'muchacho', agitated, was talking with the guide, pointing in our direction. The bus driver looked up and I could see his expression turn to dismay as he surveyed us…than the crocodile. I dared to follow his glare. The last of the crocodile, the tip of his tail, had just submerged. I tensed, knowing the reptile's swimming capabilities exceeded ours. I refocused my attention back toward the shore. We were less than ten feet away compared to his seventy-five. We were going to make it—or so I dared to hope!

Juan loaded all the passengers into the bus, then started the engine. I began to panic again, thinking he was going to leave us. I started to yell in protest but was drowned out by the sound of the horn. He wasn't leaving, he was helping, trying to distract the beast from turning us into dinner. The crocodile emerged, his large head swaying toward the source of the noise. The hunter distracted, floated as he contemplated his next move.

We were almost at the shoreline. Madoc pushed me ahead, full force, giving the extra boost I needed to reach the shoreline faster. Exiting the water as rapidly as I could, I slipped and fell on some slick, moss-covered boulders. I struggled to get up. Madoc scooped me in his arms—the third time since we'd met—and headed for the bus. I looked back at the water and saw the crocodile had lost interest, returning to sun himself at his original spot; we'd escaped.

Reaching the bus, everyone applauded and cheered, and all I could do was laugh—an unusual coping mechanism I'd inherited from my mom. Madoc looked at me curiously, shrugged, and hugged me so tightly I lost my breath. "I would never let anything happen to you! Ever!"

In that very moment…I knew I was in love. And from the look in Madoc's eyes…the feeling was mutual.

Epilogue

THREE MONTHS LATER, I GAVE UP MY CONDO IN NEW York and moved to Wisconsin so I could be closer to my newfound love. We decided to pool our money and bought a three-bedroom house—already talking about having a family—the two extra bedrooms were going to come in handy.

Our new home was in a small bedroom community north of St. Cloud, just outside of Milwaukee. For obvious reasons, we'd decided not to settle in St. Cloud. Jayson still lived in the community, although not with his family. He was renting a basement apartment in his friend's house, who was also a divorced pilot. They suffered the same weaknesses and had lost their families because of it.

Life had humbled Jayson. Annabelle was asking for a divorce, he only had weekend visits with his children, and he was currently on probation at work due to accusations of sexual misconduct. A handful of the flight attendants had somehow found out about his ledger and were not happy about it. Madoc never did give Jayson his beating, thinking karma had given him a good beating in his stead.

Madoc was still piloting flights to Mexico on a regular basis, although with a new pilot, and since I hadn't decided on a definite career path yet, I'd signed myself up for three university classes. My parents were happy I was finally pursuing an education, and my mother was even happier because I was coupled with an unmarried man.

The classes were interesting, but I wasn't sure if I wanted a degree. What I did know with absolute certainty—I didn't want to return to waitressing. Serving alcohol to drunks and spending my evenings away from Madoc didn't appeal to me at all. A job like the Chic Chick had been great at the time, but I was at a different stage in my life now, preferring the home life over the night life.

As for continuing my career as a mistress for hire . . . we knew I found the work rewarding. Madoc was proud of me but hoped I'd consider a safer job. Clearly, we both knew the risks after the incident with Jayson. We agreed continuing wasn't an option. I signed up for classes, hoping my studies would provide some clarity on a suitable career path. Money wasn't an issue. Madoc got paid enough for both of us.

My life was back to being carefree and simple again . . . until I received an e-mail.

I'd just said good-bye to Madoc. We'd embraced in the doorway for a long while before I kissed him good-bye. He was headed to work and wouldn't be back for four days. Although he was gone for several days at a time, he was rewarded with equal days off. The time away from each other only made our hearts grow fonder. I waved good-bye as he drove off and in return he flashed one of those brilliant smiles that always melted my heart.

We'd just made love and the smell of his cologne was rooted in my Gators t-shirt. I still had it, the same t-shirt I'd worn the last day I'd seen Chloe. I'd contemplated throwing it away, but it was comfortable, so I'd kept it to lounge around the house.

I went to the kitchen, poured myself a cup of coffee, and headed to the computer room. I'd neglected my studies for the four days Madoc had been home, so there was catching up to do. I flipped open my laptop and went straight to my emails. My business professor always sent the required reading electronically—she didn't like using textbooks.

I had several new messages. I found the one I was looking for and went to click on it, but before I did, I noticed I had an e-mail from an unknown address. It happened every so often. It was usually another wife, looking for my help. Curious, I opened it.

> Dear Bree,
>
> I am sending you this e-mail in hopes it finds you well.
>
> I have received positive feedback as to the service you provide.
>
> I need your assistance.
>
> My husband's name is Adam and I believe he is cheating on me.
>
> I need your help. We live in Port Hope, Seattle.
>
> Regards, Wendy K

My stomach was in knots and I felt the urge to vomit. It was Adam's *wife*—It had to be! I knew his wife's name was

Wendy and his last name was Knowles. They lived in the tiny town of Port Hope, Seattle, which only had a population of 1,500 people. And he was a cheater. I knew this all too well.

The rest of the day, I was a mess and couldn't focus on my studies. The e-mail had ignited something inside me. Something for which I still wanted answers. I couldn't help but wonder, *was he still with his other mistress? The same one he'd cheated with on me? Why did I even care? Had I maybe subconsciously created a box I didn't realize existed?*

Four days passed and I was still thinking about Adam. Madoc was set to come home that night and I welcomed his presence. I was desperate to stop thinking about my ex-lover. If anything could cease the insanity inside my brain it was Madoc.

Madoc arrived home late and I pounced on him before he'd made it through the door. We made passionate love and after we'd finished I nestled into his chest. I finally felt at peace laying in his arms.

Then it happened . . . as Madoc slept soundly beside me, my head on his chest, thoughts of Adam crept into my head, filling every space available, like sardines in a can.

Clearly, I'd hidden a box for Adam, burying it deep down, just as my mother had done. Listening to Madoc's heartbeat, I wondered, *did I still have feelings for Adam? Was I really in love with Madoc?* Touching Madoc's cheek, I contemplated waking him, wanting to share the content of the e-mail and my sentiments towards it. But instead, feeling guilty for my thoughts, I rolled over, pulling myself away from Madoc—silently I cried myself to sleep.

The next morning after Madoc left for the gym I paced around the house, mulling over Adam, not knowing what to do. I needed more coffee to help me think. I reached into the cupboard for the grounds, distracted by my thoughts, not noticing the lid was loose. The dark powder spilled down the front of my shirt and onto the floor. I started to brush the powder off the Gators logo, not wanting it to stain, when the idea came to me . . . CHLOE!

It was time for the call I had been longing to make.

I dialed Chloe's number. Although we hadn't spoken in months, I still had it memorized. I'd called it so many times over the years it was permanently etched in my brain.

"Hello, Bree?" I could hear the surprise in Chloe's tone.

I was happy to hear her voice, but I got straight to the point. "I believe you owe me a favor? I'm looking to cash in, I need you to go to Seattle with *me*."

Without the slightest hesitation she eagerly agreed, saying, "Consider it done!"

I had one more job to do but this time Chloe would be taking the lead, oh how the tables had turned! With her aid I was determined to help my ex-lover's wife. I owed it to her. But most of all, selfishly, I was determined to find out . . .

Was I still in love with Adam?

Acknowledgements

FIRSTLY, I'D LIKE TO THANK *YOU* FOR PURCHASING my book and I hope you enjoyed Bree's adventures as she embarked on her unique career path as a mistress for hire. I have enjoyed bringing Bree's character to life and look forward to continuing her story in a second book.

Secondly, I'd like to thank my inner voice/higher power/ universal energy (she goes by many names) for inspiring me to write this book and giving me the determination to complete it! I listened, and she provided, guiding me word by word, page by page. Because of her strength, not mine, I am dedicating half of the proceeds of my book to charitable organizations—my way of saying thank-you to her for the positive universal energy she bestowed on me during the time I was writing *Mistress for Hire*.

Finally, I'd like to thank my husband and children, who were patient when I assured them, "I'll only be one more hour" only to find myself hours later at the keyboard still typing away. Also, to my mom, who patiently helped with the editing. To my friends (particularly Janet for the advice), family, and co-workers who encouraged me along the way and the team at Friesen Press Publishing (Ellie,

Teresita, Oriana and Lisa), who were amazing, supporting me through my first book and making it a success.

Smiles,
Abby Parker

About The Author

Abby Parker resides in Canada with her husband and three children. A law enforcement officer by profession, she writes for the love of it. Abby enjoys charity work and recently led a project to build a police station in Africa. Abby aspires to continue her humanitarian work and donate half the proceeds of her book, *Mistress for Hire*, towards these efforts. In her spare time, she enjoys bee keeping, traveling, playing ringette, and spending time with family and friends.

Printed in Canada